Ian Macpherson

Bluemoose

First published in 2019 by
Bluemoose Books Ltd
25 Sackville Street
Hebden Bridge
West Yorkshire
HX7 7DJ

www.bluemoosebooks.com

British Library Cataloguing-in-Publication data
A catalogue record for this book is available from the British Library

Paperback 978-1-910422-53-3

Printed and bound in the UK by Short Run Press

'Are you a sloot? Are you, Hayding?' – *The three aunts*

To my beloved daughters
Rosie and Maeve

1

Hayden couldn't see the audience from the stage. He didn't *want* to see the audience from the stage. He wanted to be at home writing his novel – not that he'd started it yet – but there he was, caught in the unforgiving glare of the spotlight.

He'd just launched into an alcohol-related riff about a lost weekend in Scrabster with the bass player from the Clits. An extended shaggy-dog story about picking up all the bacchanalian details from the subsequent court case. He'd told it once too often and the audience fed off his lethargy. Result? A smattering of confused laughter, as if they didn't quite know why they were laughing.

Hayden McGlynn was good-looking in a louche sort of way. Bit like me. The words dry, laconic, cerebral might best describe his comic schtick. No harm in that, you might say, but it's not to everyone's taste. This particular night he was getting away with it. Just. The venue, Old Joanna's, is situated near Kentish Town tube in one of London's trendier areas. Bespoke bookshops. Designer charity shops. Greengrocers with hand-crafted okra. With matching audience. Which explained why Hayden hadn't been howled offstage. Yet.

He abandoned the sorry tale with a heavily edited ending and was about to segue into a routine about discovering he wasn't Jewish – the only penis reference in his entire act – when a lone voice from the sea of darkness before him interrupted. 'I've just had a great idea,' it suggested drily. 'Why don't you say something funny?' Cruel but, in the merciless world of comedy, fair. The audience, as if suddenly freed from the shackles of civilised behaviour, hooted. A genuine, from-the-heart eruption of unrestrained glee. And with that eruption, Hayden was cast into the seventh circle of standup hell. Laughter, yes, but the wrong sort. Every comedian's nightmare. At, not with. The audience stared at him for an eternity. No. Hold on. It felt like an eternity to him. But to them, with their comfy seats, and their safety in numbers, and the womb-like darkness of the room, it was less than the time it takes to read this line.

He leaned into the mic with a professional nonchalance he didn't totally feel. 'Sorry,' he said, 'it's my ad lib writer's day off.'

Laughter. He'd risen to the challenge – for now. Now, in the best scientific definition available, being one nanosecond on either side of the present. But now moved on. The voice from the darkness was back.

'Well, what do you think he'd say if he *was* here?'

Hayden was ready for this. This one was easy. This one was a gift. '*She'd* say "How's that for a lightning-quick sex change?"' He rode the wave of laughter and, at exactly the right point, held his hand up for silence. '"You've never met me," she'd continue, "so what led you to assume I was male in the first place?"'

Applause. Laughter. No retaliation. He was almost back on top. But where to from here? He couldn't count on members of the audience giving him feeder lines ad infinitum, so back into the act, that was where! And he'd make it sound like he'd never said any of it before.

'When I was twelve I was convinced I was –'

'Jewish. Heard it.'

'Haven't we all.'

Laughter reflecting their own cleverness back at themselves, the okra-munching fucks. Hayden's thoughts, by the way, not mine. They were taunting him now. If Hayden was denied the safety net of his overworked material, he had to match them quip for quip. The audience knew this and had moved in for the kill.

All that would save Hayden now from blood on the floor was a deus ex machina, and at precisely the moment of maximum need, his mobile rang in his left trouser pocket. 'Ode to Joy': the ice-cream van version. The timing was immaculate. Had the gods caught on to modern technology? Gods or no gods, it worked.

'Put it on loudspeaker,' a female voice called from the distance. 'We'll close our eyes and pretend it's a radio play.'

A burst of laughter gave Hayden time to think. Worth a shot. He glanced at the screen. Bram. His oldest and best friend. Bus driver on the 130 route, City Centre to Clontarf, Dublin 3. He stared into the middle distance and pressed accept.

'Bram.'

Murmurs of approval. The audience settled in. Imaginary cup of tea. Biscuit. Dagger at the ready.

'I know,' quipped the phone in a Dublin accent, the mic catching and amplifying it perfectly.

Audience laughter. Hayden braced himself. He didn't know where this was going.

The audience remained settled. Sup of tea. Quick biscuit-dunk. Dagger disguised as a cake knife.

'Listen, Bram, I'm onstage at the moment.' He draped an arm over the mic-stand and feigned serene.

'Good man yourself. I'll tell you something. You wouldn't get *me* up there. So, how's it going?'

Hayden opted for acerbic. 'Since you ask,' he said, 'I was holding it together pretty well till about 20 seconds ago.'

'Could be your gags,' said Bram.

The audience tittered. They would have hooted, but they didn't want to miss anything, because this was good. This was *very* good.

Bram spoke through the titters. 'Here's one you can use, right? There's this –'

Hayden cut across him. 'Bad time, Bram.'

'Fair enough. Leave it to the pros. I take it you'll be coming over.'

'No plans at the moment, no.'

Bram's pause sounded surprised. 'Ri-i-ight,' he said. 'I'll pass on your condolences so. Catch you later. Oh, and before I go. Might be an idea to call the aunts.'

With that he was gone. The audience wasn't. You could almost feel them coalesce for the sheer joy of mischief.

'For pity's sake, man, take us out of our misery. Call the aunts.' A single voice.

'Call the aunts.' A smattering of voices.

'Call the aunts.' The entire, electrified room.

'Call the aunts! Call the aunts! Call the aunts!' A metronomic pounding of feet on the floor like one giant foot. This was getting dangerously close to Nuremberg '38.

Hayden bowed to the inevitable. He peered at the screen. Tapped in a number. Listened to the familiar buzzing sound as the number connected.

The audience settled back.

Pause.

'Howaya, Hayding.'

'It's your tree aunties here. In Dubling.'

'Course we didn't need to say that.'

'Being as how *you* phoned *us.*'

The audience erupted. It was something about the tone. Tiny voices. High-pitched. Ancient as history.

'We're getting static here, Hayding.'

'Maybe if you moved a bit closer.'

'Like the Isle of Man.'

The audience, loving every second of it, shushed.

'Tanks, Hayding. That's miles better.'

'But might we say you're not easy to get hold of, pardonnez our French.'

'We tried *everyting.*'

'Old address.'

'Spiritualism.'

'Divine intervention.'

'Nutting.'

'So tanks for phoning. You're a *very* good boy.'

'I think you'll find that was our idea,' an indignant voice shouted from the darkness. This heartfelt interjection, followed by laughter, set the three aunts off on a tangent.

'You've got company, Hayding.'

'A little friend, perhaps?'

'Only we do be worried about you all on your ownio over there in the great big metropolis.'

'Wit its mighty beating heart.'

'And its mighty beating –'

Hayden coughed for dramatic effect. 'Thing is, I'm onstage at the moment,' he said.

'Aren't you great dough, Hayding. *Very* brave.'

A round of ironic applause.

'And popular too, if we may make so bold.'

The audience roared. The three aunts could do no wrong.

'See, Hayding? You got a big laugh there and you never said a ting.'

'But timing is very important in comedy, Hayding, and you're a bit late for the silent fillums. You could've been *huge*.'

Wild, spontaneous applause.

'See? There you go again.'

'But we digress.'

'Do we?'

'Yes, Dottie. We do.'

'Florrie. You're Dottie. We were wondering, Hayding, if you were coming back for the funerdle.'

'Funerdle?' The audience was back on a point of information. 'Ask them who died!'

'Did we not say, Hayding? Uncle Eddie.'

'So anyway. Are you coming over for the funerdle?'

2

Without the three aunts to back him, Hayden was stuck with his act. He slipped the mobile into his back pocket and steeled himself. He knew what was coming next. So, it seemed, did the audience. Maybe it was the way he held the mic, or maybe it was the merest hint of weariness behind the eyes. Hayden braced himself.

'The –'

'Heard it.'

Laughter. Theirs, not his. He raised a hand in mock triumph.

'So have I. You've been a wonderful audience. Irony intended. Goodnight.'

He left the stage to teasing whoops and the odd word of encouragement: 'Hope you get more laughs at the funerdle.' A sympathetic squeeze from the compère as he brushed past. A dismissive thumbs-up from baby-faced, spindly-legged Foetus O'Flaherty as he bounded, no introduction needed, onstage.

FOETUS (ECSTATIC): Howaya!
AUDIENCE (EQUALLY ECSTATIC): Howaya!!!

Hayden may have exited to a spontaneous eruption of delight, to howls of expectant laughter, but the howls were not for him. For every standup, there's a moment where you realise you'll never get that kind of laughter again, that the world has shifted imperceptibly on its axis, and this was Hayden's moment. The generational handover moment. Nothing to be done. Move on. He opened the door at the back, slipped out, and closed it quietly on his past. The adjoining bar he now entered was his present and, by implication, the beginning of his future. A future yet to be mapped. Symbolically perhaps, it was empty.

Steve the barman stopped polishing the counter. 'Sounded like a good one, mate,' he said. 'Usual?'

Hayden nodded and grabbed a stool. Steve filled a glass with ice, tossed in a lemon slice, and placed it meticulously on the bar. As he bent to open the cooler, the performance door opened. A woman came out as the audience erupted. She hesitated, then headed towards Hayden. A superannuated waif, with sad eyes and light brown hair that didn't know what to do with itself, she frowned as Hayden moodily fingered his glass. Steve reappeared, whisked the top off a bottle and poured it, with a flourish, into Hayden's glass. Sparkling water. The woman relaxed slightly. Hayden burrowed in his pocket. Steve raised his hand.

'On the house,' he said. 'And what is your young lady's pleasure?'

Hayden looked confused.

'It's Trace, remember?' she said, easing herself onto the barstool beside him. She smiled shyly at Steve. 'I'll have what Hayden's having.'

Hayden swivelled discreetly on his stool, just a few degrees away from her, as if erecting a psychological barrier of sorts. He knew this woman. But how? Where? Why? She certainly seemed to know him.

'You were magic tonight,' she said. He wasn't. 'They just didn't understand you,' she said. They did.

Hayden stared into his glass, his silence drowned out by whoops from the other room. Foetus had already whipped the audience up into a frenzy with his call-and-response catchphrase.

'Hey, fella, where you from?'

'Termonfeckin!'

'Yow!'

'Funny guy,' said Steve. He rinsed a glass that didn't need rinsing and leaned over to Trace. 'Had a chat with him earlier. Turns out the midwife called him Little Foetus. His mum thought Foetus was an Irish saint.' He shook with internalised merriment.

Hayden bristled. 'Hilarious, Steve,' he said. 'His name is Fergus.'

This was a classic case of a standup pulling rank. Steve was a great barman, the sort who seemed to have time for everyone, but he'd made a basic error: he found another comedian funny. Steve winced. Might be best, he thought, to change the subject.

'So, when did you two – you know.'

Hayden rolled his glass as if it contained the finest malt, and took a tentative sip.

'An AA meeting,' said Trace.

Of course! Hayden had gone to one AA meeting. Emphasis on the one. Big mistake.

'Our eyes met across a crowded room,' said Trace.

They had too, thought Hayden. Sometimes people's eyes meet across a crowded room because they happen to be facing each other at the time and the people in between are sitting down. But Trace was cursed with the romantic gene. She'd read things into it.

'I sensed his...' She smiled and sighed softly, a misty glow in her eyes. 'I dunno, *vulnerability*?' He hadn't been vulnerable. He'd been sober. 'I thought he needed looking after. Except he never came back, so here I am, doing my duty by the Higher Power. You know. Just keeping an eye on things.' She beamed at him. 'And isn't he doing great?'

Hayden faced into the bar and stared at the row of spirits. But no. He wouldn't be drawn. He was off the stuff for good. No lapses so far, though he had to admit real life was a bit hard to take, and there was so much of it. But maybe that was the point: at least you got to experience it. As if reading his thoughts, Steve decided to guide the conversation elsewhere.

'That stuff about the Clits,' he said. 'Is it, like, *true*?'

Hayden took a meditative swig from his glass. Interesting watery notes. Aquatic tones. Hint of bubble.

'I don't know,' he said. He thought about expanding on this. No court case, but he *had* woken up with the bass player from the Clits. True story, embellished for comic effect. So the story wasn't, perhaps, factually accurate. On the other hand it was artistically true, so Hayden left it at that. Trace, however, didn't.

'Thing is,' she said, 'if you'd been sober you wouldn't've done it. Whatever it is.'

Hayden shrugged. 'I probably didn't do it anyway,' he said.

'But you'd've *known* you hadn't done it,' said an infuriatingly emollient Trace. 'Besides, *God* knows. And He's really chuffed that you've stuck with His Twelve Point Plan.'

Hayden grabbed his glass and slammed it down on a beer mat. 'Twelve Point Plan? God? What the hell does this non-existent God of yours know about alcohol, me, and what I got up to in, in, in *Scrabster* with his Twelve Point fucking Plan?'

Steve winced. It wasn't the God bit, or the swearing. He'd heard all that before. He slid the beer mat discreetly to one side and inspected the copper counter. No dent. He relaxed and thought about intervening, but Trace got there first. She gave Hayden a pleading look.

Hayden drained his glass and sat it, gently this time, back on the bar. 'Okay, look, sorry,' he said. 'But give me a break. A man can only take so much.' He glanced at his watch. 'Anyway, got to go. Lots to do. You know. Things. Other things.'

'Good to know,' said Steve. 'Like what?'

'Well,' said Hayden, 'packing for a start.' He probably should have left it there. 'Oh, and I'm writing a novel, actually.'

He'd meant to keep it to himself, at least until he'd written the opening line. But there it was. Out. Steve nodded his approval.

'Smart move,' he said. 'What's it about?'

'Early days yet,' said Hayden. Steve gave him a questioning look, so he felt the need to elaborate. 'Bit hush hush.' So hush hush even he didn't know.

Steve leaned in closer. 'I'll tell you one thing,' he said. 'Crime fiction. That's where the money's at.' He polished the counter lovingly. 'If I was you, I'd go straight for the genre stuff. You'd never have to work again.'

Hayden sat up. 'That,' he lied, 'is *exactly* what I'm writing.' This was his eureka moment. Why hadn't *he* thought of it? He had to claim ownership of the idea, and he had to do it now! 'Comedy crime, Steve,' he said, settling back on his stool like a seasoned pro. 'Well done. Got it in one. You can't go wrong with a corpse, right?' He was talking to himself at this point. 'You sit at home, happily tapping it out, and here's the beauty of it: you get all the adulation without the hassle of that lot.' He pointed back in the general direction of the now hysterical audience, muted behind the closed door. 'Early days as I say, but I do know this. It's funny. It's crime. It's sort of, I dunno, black comedy.'

'You said it, brother.'

'Not that sort of black, Steve,' said Hayden. 'Sort of Celtic screwball noir. New genre.'

'Bejasus now. Put me down for a copy. So where are you headed?'

'Sorry?'

'You said you were packing.'

'Dublin,' said Trace. Hayden sighed. He realised there were downsides to sharing your phone calls onstage. Trace shot him a sidelong glance. 'Whereabouts?'

What sort of question was that?

'Different bits,' he said. 'All depends where I am at the time.'

Steve nodded sagely. 'Makes sense,' he said. 'How long?'

'Couple of nights tops,' said Hayden. 'Maybe three.'

Steve leaned across the counter and dropped his voice. 'A word to the wise,' he said. 'Underpants.'

Hayden arched an eyebrow and paused for effect. 'Underpants.'

'Three nights, two pairs? Bad,' said Steve. 'Vice versa? Good. Trust me. I speak from bitter experience.'

'I'll bear that in mind,' said Hayden as he pushed his stool back. He nodded to Steve, waved a half-hearted farewell to Trace, and left the bar. Steve reached into the cooler for another bottle of sparkling water. Trace stared wistfully at the counter.

'Well anyway,' she said softly as Steve placed a fresh glass in front of her. 'He's doing just great.'

Next door the audience hooted.

Hayden lived close to the venue, just off Kentish Town Road. It was a hot summer night. The pavement teemed with the chemically ecstatic, so he sweltered home in the gutter, the memory of his performance still rankling and raw. True, he was going to write his breakout novel, but that was still at the pre-embryonic stage and besides, the best idea so far had come from someone else.

So this was what it had come to. At forty-three, he was old and – literally, if the gutter was anything to go by – in the way. He let himself in to his tiny bedsit. Two-ring stove. Fold-up bed. No visitors. Visitors were allowed; they just wouldn't fit.

He closed the door on the outside world. He was still old but no longer in the way, which was better, but not much. A letter from his landlord lay crumpled on the folded-down fold-up bed. I won't repeat it in full; too painful. Here's the gist: *We've decided to triple the rent, because we care.* Hayden tossed it on the floor and crashed down on the bed. Cue age- and career-related depression. Fortunately, his mobile came to the rescue. He glanced at the screen. His agent.

'Ay!'

'Dickie!'

'Black mark, Ay. Name's Rich.'

Hayden wasn't having this. 'While we're on the subject, *Rich*, my name is Hayden. Two syllables. With a H.'

'With you, Ay. Anyway. Gravesend. Tuesday. You to headline, don't-ask-me-why. New promoter, shit taste? Whatever. Great support act. Kid from, wait for it –'

'He'll be supporting himself, Rich. Can't do it. I'm dealing with a bereavement at the moment.'

'Your career?'

'Plus –' and Hayden shouldn't have said this but he did '– I'm writing a novel, actually.'

Damn. 'Actually' again. He had to cut it out. Luckily, Rich ignored it. He was already thinking money.

'Call me Mister 25% on any – wait for it – fillum deals. Get it? Fillum?' Hayden said nothing. He got it. 'This novel, Ay. Any good?'

'Haven't started yet, but –'

'Oh, *that* writing a novel. I've got one of those on the go myself.'

Hayden sighed at the ceiling. 'Much as I'd like to chat all night, *Dick*,' he said, 'I've decided I'd prefer, on balance, to sit alone in a darkened room and decompose.'

This was followed by a three-second pause, which threw Hayden. He'd never experienced a pause with Rich before. Time was money. Maybe, at last, he'd got through to his empathetic side.

'You've never really made it, 'ave you, Ay?'

Hayden searched the tone for empathy and didn't find any. He didn't have to press End Call. Rich had done that for him. He put his mobile down and grabbed a blank notebook. He'd begin his novel here, and he'd begin it now. Celtic screwball noir. He untopped his biro and opened the notebook.

The blank notebook.

Three hours later it was still blank.

3

As a writer, I'm always happy to travel, and where better than Dublin? My home town! So when Hayden decided to take a couple of days' respite from the real world and attend Eddie's funeral, I thought, why not follow him over? Describe his journey, *ex* and *in*ternal. And I'm very glad I did.

What unfolds over the coming pages follows the archetypal 'overcoming the demons' narrative which has existed in popular fiction since humans' earliest attempts at plot structure. Who, for instance, hasn't watched in joyous wonder as the small boy with motor neurone disease overcomes every obstacle, including a working-class father with traditional values, to dance the pas de deux with the Royal Ballet and make the front cover of Vanity Fair – all before the age of six – as lovely Gloria Crump? Bit like that with *Sloot*. It ends on a triumphant note, so relax. Happy ending guaranteed.

Hayden also tackles his own crime novel with surprising results. Think of it as a book within a book, and rather him than me to write it, to be honest. Don't get me wrong – I love crime fiction, but it's not as easy as it looks. I should know. I've tried, several times. The secret? Plot, plot, plot. Unfortunately, my ability to tell a gripping story was effectively killed off at an impressionable age. I was seventeen. I went to university. I fell under the dubious influence of the postmodernists, in particular *How to Write an Experimental Novel That Doesn't Sell and Keeps on Not Selling,* by – actually, you don't want to know. Forget I said it. That way madness lies.

But said malign influence helps to explain the structure of this book. At its heart, an accidental detective who'd rather write his own Celtic screwball noir than solve the crime, and a narrator who loses the plot. Literally. Sound complicated? Not so. Thanks to a revolutionary narrative structure of the author's own devising, The Inquisitive Bullet, it's simplicity itself. I've also adapted certain aphorisms attributed, I believe, to Sigmund Freud. 'If you introduce a cigar in Act One,' for instance, 'make sure you smoke it in Act Three.'

Where was I? Dublin and, more specifically, Clontarf. Perfect. I grew up in that leafy suburb myself. Mother. Father. Siblings. I could happily have dispensed with the latter but what can you do? People *will* breed. Childhood overall was a happy experience, for me at least. Not so for Hayden. His parents moved from Clontarf to Honolulu on the eve of his seventh birthday. Something about job opportunities. They live in Honolulu to this day. His mother runs the Celtic Studies department at Waikiki College of Higher Education, his father writes a regular column for the Irish Times about living with a woman who runs the Celtic Studies Department at Waikiki College of Higher Education. No mention of Hayden, though. He was farmed out to his three aunts and Uncle Eddie. Why? And how did this sudden wrench, at such an impressionable age, affect Hayden?

The short answer is that he took it surprisingly well. His parents had always been a bit cold and distant. Following the move they were still cold, and doubly distant. They feature in Hayden's story, but only towards the end of Chapter 32, and only as catalysts for a plot twist so audacious I still blink in slack-jawed awe when I bring it to the forefront of my mind.

4

While I've been filling you in on these sniblets of crucial information, the plot has been bubbling away nicely in the background. Hayden has bought the cheapest plane ticket available, cancelled a gig in Morden, gone to the airport, touched down in Dublin. He's also, after much dithering, packed three pairs of underpants, including the ones he's got on. An unnecessary detail? Not so. As with cigars, so with underpants.

But I digress. Hayden. Airport. There to meet him in the arrivals hall was his oldest and best friend, Bram. They played together as children. Went to school together. Primary school, secondary school. Then the inevitable parting of the ways. Bram to Bus Eireann, Hayden to university and the heady joys of exile. But still the friendship endured; possibly more nostalgic attachment than actual friendship by now, but even so. Your best friend is your best friend and Bram, in this case, was his.

Hardly a word passed between the two men as they made their way to the car. Bram strolled on ahead with Hayden's shoulder bag while Hayden examined the back of his head. It had aged considerably since he'd been over last. Hayden put it at — what? Five years' absence? Six? He couldn't put a precise date on it. The past was an alcohol-fuelled blur, but since his last visit Bram had developed a bald spot, and what had been a profusion of black curls in his youth now grew wispy and grey. Hayden, having the narcissistic streak of all comedians, was wondering about the back of his own head. Was he developing a bald spot too? He knew he was turning grey, but he didn't like the thought of wispy. It was a small step from wispy to frail to...

Bram clicked the car lock from a distance with a flourish. He was old enough to remember keys you stuck into things, and the novelty hadn't entirely worn off.

'Welcome back,' he said. 'You haven't changed a bit.'

'I really should get back more often,' said Hayden. 'I mean, it's been what? *Years.*'

Bram looked at him quizzically. 'Right,' he said. 'Certainly seems that way.' He started the ignition and moved off. 'So, how's the career?'

Hayden settled back in his seat. 'I'm writing a novel, actually,' he said.

'Brilliant,' said Bram. 'When's it out?'

'Early days yet,' said Hayden.

Bram nodded. 'Enough said.'

Silence. Bram concentrated on the traffic. Hayden struggled with his ego and lost. 'It's a crime thriller,' he said.

Bram glanced over with a new respect. 'Good man yourself,' he said. 'Big fan of the old crime genre. Big fan. Tried one myself a while back. To be honest, it was probably a mistake making him a lady cop. And setting it in Malmö. Never been to Norway. Who's your main man?'

'I'm still working on that,' said Hayden.

Bram nodded and pointed towards the back of the car. 'See that box on the back seat?' he said. 'Tons of hard-boiled paperbacks for Oxfam. Hold on to them if you like. Might come in handy, you know? Research.' He whacked the steering wheel, animated. 'Grab hold of one there.' Hayden resigned himself to a Bram monologue, reached back and took one off the top of the pile. 'Go on,' said Bram. 'Hit me.'

'*An American Toddler,*' read Hayden.

Bram gave it the thumbs up. 'Good one. Child psycho. Little Charlton. Blows his ma away with her own gun. Can't be held culpable at age three. No charge. We're talking Land of the Free here, right? So, he starts popping other people's mammies. Contract stuff. Screw you to the judge; he's got the gun lobby behind him. I won't spoil the ending for you. I think that cowboy actor fella's directing the screen version. Next?'

'Tell you what,' said Hayden. 'I'll have a look later. Don't want to clutter the head.'

'Fair point,' said Bram. 'Maybe that's why I never got anywhere myself. Read all the books, read all the how-to manuals, never got past the opening line. I knew who dunnit, but I didn't know why he dunnit. Or, come to think of it, what he dunn. Make sense?'

'Not really, no,' said Hayden. 'And Malmö is in Sweden.'

Bram mulled this over as if it made a difference. He seemed to be going the wrong way for the cemetery, but Hayden didn't like to intervene. Besides, they were heading towards Clontarf, and Hayden was feeling nostalgic.

'Okay,' said Bram. 'First rule of crime fiction: Know Thy Perp. Perp is Scandinavian for culprit. Anyway, if you know who perped the crime you work backwards, planting clues as you go, till you reach the beginning. That way, when the reader reaches the end, it's all totally logical. You're left thinking, should've seen that one coming, couldn't have been anyone else.'

Interestingly enough, thought Hayden, that does make sense. Maybe Bram was an idiot savant after all. 'I'll make a mental note,' he said. 'Anything else?'

Bram looked pleased with himself. He seemed to have grown in stature in his own head. 'Second rule,' he said. 'Your hero, the guy who's looking for the guy who dunnit, right? He has a flaw.'

'What?' said Hayden. 'Like he's a woman?'

'That's not a flaw,' said Bram. 'Is it?'

'Joke, Bram,' said Hayden. 'Go on.'

Bram was on a roll. 'He's got a thicko sidekick. The talk-to guy. That way he keeps the readers up to speed through someone who's even thicker than they are.'

'Good point,' said Hayden. 'Bit like life, eh?' Bram looked over at him, puzzled. Hayden, thinking pile-up, changed tack. 'This is good stuff, Bram. Big help.'

Relaxing, Bram turned his attention back to the road. 'At your service,' he said. 'Can't help you with the opening line, though.'

'Leave that to me, Bram. I'll run it past you when I get there. Why are we stopping here?'

They'd taken a detour via Coolock and Vernon Avenue, past Mac's sweetie shop, Madden's Supermarket, Menton's, Sullivan's, The Nook. Left at the sea front. Stop.

'The Nautical Buoy, Haydo. It's been refurbished. I thought you might fancy a quick pint before the do.'

'It's not a do, Bram. It's a funeral. We don't have time. And I don't drink.'

'Ah. Right. Because of – you know?'

'No, Bram. I don't know.'

'You know. The incident that dare not speak its name.'

'What incident? You mean Scrabster?'

Bram nodded. A conspiratorial nod. 'If you say so. Scrabster it is.' A pregnant pause. 'Half? Glass of wine?'

'Great to be back,' said Hayden. 'Sobriety and the Irish: discuss.'

As he said it, a distinguished-looking drunk in a fedora lurched out of the Nautical Buoy and spilled into a taxi.

'Funny,' said Bram, 'I could almost swear that's your man.'

Hayden thought he recognised him from somewhere but he had other calls on his time. 'If we don't get a move on,' he said, 'we'll be late.'

'I'm a bus driver,' said Bram. 'It's my job to be late.'

'Brilliant,' said Hayden. 'Mind if I use that?'

'Really?' said Bram.

'No, not really,' said Hayden. He patted Bram affectionately on the shoulder. 'Drive on.'

Bram drove on in silence. Bus driver silence. Thinking bus driver thoughts. Hayden embraced the imaginary glass partition and watched Dublin fly past. Its roads. Its houses. Its people. They arrived at Glasnevin Cemetery late. Bus driver late. Bram drove slowly through the gates and parked the car.

'I went to the laying in, by the way,' he said. 'Took a shot of Eddie for you on the mobile. Very peaceful. I suppose he would be though. You know. What with him being dead.'

5

Inside the crematorium the rows were full of mourners. Hayden and Bram stood unobtrusively at the back. Hayden spent most of the funeral service thinking about his own mortality and putting faces to the backs of people's heads. Did he know them? Had they aged? Was the back of his own head bald? And who was the statuesque, imposing woman in the last row? He certainly didn't know her, and he wasn't about to find out. As the celebrant droned to a halt and Eddie's coffin trundled towards the incinerator, she stood up suddenly, turned and, with eyes obscured behind a half-veil, walked briskly towards the exit.

As she brushed past Hayden their eyes met – as much as eyes can be said to meet behind a half-veil. There was something unnerving about her. Hayden considered following her out and observing her from a discreet distance, but something stopped him. Possibly fear. His mouth was certainly dry and she didn't look like the sort of woman you'd mess with. Contained. Assured-looking. Well-endowed shoulders. Doubly striking in funeral black. He chose to stay and deconstruct her where he was. The intellectual's way out. Eddie, meanwhile, disappeared from view and the mourners stood up slowly and shuffled out. Hayden, lost in thought, shuffled with them.

Outside the crematorium were men with hands buried deep in trouser pockets and women checking their mobiles. The usual funeral banalities; until, that is, Hayden's nonagenarian aunts doddered into view. Three tiny little heads bobbing about as if with one body, like a benevolent hydra.

'Will you look who it is.'

'Howaya, stranger.'

'Haven't seen you in yonks.'

'Longer than yonks *I'd* say.'

'Well that all depends how long a yonk *is*, Dodie.'

'Dottie. Anyway, nice to see you back for the funerdle, Hayding.'

'And will you look at young Abraham.'

'Hasn't he got very big?'

'Plus, it hasn't escaped our attention in spite of our great age and concomitant waning powers, he's wearing longers.'

Bram gave them a puzzled look. He hadn't worn short trousers for decades. And his name wasn't Abraham.

'So how are tings in Londinium, Hayding?'

'That's what it was called when *we* were over first. Young ladies in our prime.'

'Awful sad though, isn't it?'

Hayden was confused. 'What is?'

'Eddie. Our dear departed little brudder. To go like that, you know?'

'In *his* prime.'

'Eighty-six. So young. So young.'

One of them, possibly Florrie, poked Hayden on his hip bone.

'Did you see the mysterious lady at the back, Hayding?'

'His secret lover, you possibly surmise?'

They moved in closer.

'All is not as it seems, Hayding.'

'We'll go furder. *She's* not all she seems.'

'How so?' he said, humouring them. It was a funeral after all, and they weren't long for this world themselves. Besides, he was very fond of them in his own undemonstrative way, so it was the least he could do.

'Oh now. It's more than our lives are wort.'

'Our lips, Hayding, are permulently sealed.'

'You should have seen him, dough.'

'Him?'

'Eddie, Hayding. He looked so peaceful.'

'Beatific, almost.'

'Oh, I don't tink so, Dottie.'

'Dodie.'

'Isn't beatific religious, Hayding?'

'And he wasn't religious, Hayding. Far from it.'

'But he certingly looked very peaceful −'

'− if not beatific −'

'− at the end.'

'All laid out in his open coffing.'

'There, you'd have said, was a very −'

'I took a picture,' said Bram.

The three aunts stopped in mid-flow.

'You what?'

'On my mobile,' said Bram. 'You know. For Hayden, so he could −'

'But... you can't do that.'

'It's... what's the word?'

'Sacrilegious.'

'But Eddie wasn't religious, remember?' said Hayden. 'He wouldn't have minded.'

'Oh now. Oh *now.*'

'There's such a ting as respect for the dead.'

'*We're* not religious, Hayding, since we espoused existentialism in the mid-to-late forties −'

'− but don't go doing holiday snaps of *us* when we're on the metaphorical slab.'

'Even if we're fully made up.'

Dodie, or was it Florrie or, indeed, Dottie, snapped her fingers.

'Hand it over, young man.'

'This instant.'

Bram, suddenly six again, did as he was told. All three aunts huddled round and peered at the image on his mobile. Click.

'Deleted.'

They handed the mobile back with a distinct pursing of lips as if, by taking the image, Bram had defiled something sacred.

'Maybe now the poor man can rest in peace.'

Bram, chastened, put the mobile back in his pocket. He was pretty sure they weren't referring to him.

6

Hayden had always loved Eddie's expansive living room stroke kitchen. The way the light came in from windows to the north and south. Open plan before open plan was fashionable, because Eddie had always been an original thinker.

The room was big and shambolic, cluttered as it was – every wall, every corner, every available space – with Eddie's art works, finished and unfinished. A self-portrait of an old, mocking Eddie on one wall faced an identically-framed mirror. Over the mirror: *I have no need of recognition: I recognise myself.* A large glass case contained an enormous turnip immersed in liquid. *The Archbishop of Dublin in Formaldehyde.*

Hayden stood with Bram in the midst of all the chaos, watching absentmindedly as the three aunts fussed around the mourners, topping up their glasses, commiserating. It all passed him by in a blur. Bram was midway through a résumé of pulp classic *Talk Among Yourself,* about a private eye with multiple personality disorder, but Hayden wasn't listening. He'd shoved Bram's book box under Eddie's writing desk; he could read it himself later. Besides, he was transfixed by the Eddieness of Eddie's house. The manic creativity. The faded grandeur. The dust.

'We note you examining the surroundings wit a somewhat critical eye, Hayding.'

His aunts' voices interrupted his thoughts.

'We were going to tidy up as a mark of respect, but in the end we didn't touch a ting.'

'You just never know wit Eddie. He let the place go in his later years.'

'Or did he?'

'That cobweb on the ceiling, par example. Knowing our illustrious brudder, it could be an art installation of finest filigree.'

'But we digress, Hayding. We were discussing the contents of his will.'

'*Chun suimiú suas a dhéanamh*, we're the executrixes.'

'But we're keeping schtum till after the prostate.'

Prostate? What were they on about now? Did Eddie have posthumous cancer? No chance of interrupting the aunts in full flow. But prostate?

'We can't say anyting, Hayding, except to say we can't say anyting.'

This set them off in a fit of giggles like a flock of starlings on holiday. Bram leaned helpfully over while they were in full flight.

'I think they might mean probate.'

Of course they did. He'd been away too long.

'Anyway, Hayding, the pertinent info at this stage is as follows.'

'He wants his ashes trown to the four winds.'

'Wait for it.'

'At the Hellfire Club.'

'In the heart of his beloved Dubling Mountings.'

'On the first full-moon night after his sad demise.'

'At tree tirty-tree, Hayding. He said he was meeting ould Lucifer half-way.'

'Isn't that gas?'

'Now, can one of us top you up? We've got sherry, portofino, brandy –'

'I don't drink,' said Hayden.

The three aunts giggled as one woman.

'Try telling that to the judge.'

'Only joking, Hayding. Very commendable.'

'There's a pot of tea just made. Would you like a cup?'

'You drink *tea*, Hayding, so *technically* speaking, you *do* drink.'

'Unless he doesn't drink tea.'

'Don't be ridiculous, Florrie.'

'Dottie.'

'*Everyone* drinks tea. And even if he didn't, he'd have to drink someting. Or he'd wilt. Wouldn't you, Hayding? You'd *wilt*.'

Hayden ignored them. 'I thought I'd sleep here,' he said.

The aunts looked... difficult to describe how they looked. Worried? Disapproving? Defensive? Their eyes may have narrowed slightly. The starlings flew away.

'What? You mean overnight, Hayding?'

'But why?'

'Sure you can always stay wit us.'

'Or me,' said Bram.

'There y'are, Hayding. Abraham has spoken from on high.'

'His sofa awaits.'

'Not to mention male company and its attendant badinage.'

Bram nodded in agreement. That sounded about right.

'I want to stay here,' said Hayden. 'You know. Old times. Memories.'

'What?'

'All alone?'

'Isn't that a bit creepy?'

They scuttled off before he could answer.

Why did they not want him to stay at Eddie's? If Hayden had been more tuned in to their little ways at this point, with particular reference to the narrowing of the eyes, he would have been, at the very least, suspicious. But he wasn't. He pretended to be engrossed as Bram switched to the book he was currently reading.

'*A Killing in Killala*. Twin brothers from Dudley, both Muslim, right? They get wind of the village in County Mayo, think 'Whoa! *Kill Allah?!*' There's your inciting incident right there. It fires them up. They travel to Killala to wipe it from the face of the earth. Settle in, suicide vests at the ready. But what's this? The sleepy charm of the locals begins to have that age-old effect. They dispense with the vests and settle down. Get married. Have little Catholic babies. Become respected pillars of the community and – here's the twist – end up killing each other, in time-honoured tradition, in a bitter, fraternal feud over land. They have become, in a word, more Irish than the Irish themselves. Magic!'

Hayden nodded politely, but he was more interested in having the place to himself at this stage than listening to any more of Bram's stories. He felt the need to be alone. Besides, he was drawn to the ramshackle old house. After his parents left for Waikiki, Hayden had gone to live with his Uncle Eddie. His childhood bedroom was here, and with it, his childhood. He stood for a long moment lost in thought, feeling tearful. But he wasn't tearful for his dead uncle.

He was tearful for himself.

The sun was going down as Hayden finally closed the door on the few remaining mourners, the three aunts, and Bram. He was alone. He could have stayed at Bram's and riffled through his books. He could have stayed with his aunts and ended up killing them. Instead he sat with a cold cup of tea at the table in Eddie's living room. He sighed and looked around. What a melancholy feel to the place! Mildewed walls. The light fading. The wallpaper peeling, and what rugs covered the floorboards faded and worn.

A sudden wave of desolation washed over him. He unlocked the back door and let himself out. An adrenalin rush of happy nostalgia mingled with the sweet sea air. He'd always loved the garden. He sat on a rickety old bench and soaked in the atmosphere. Fruit trees filtering the setting summer sun. The ramshackle shed. Wild privets on both sides. Beyond the wall at the rear, a large and looming redbrick house. The overgrown grass was littered with artworks in various states of completion – in pride of place, an imposing sculpture in search of a plinth. Hayden remembered this one well. Eddie had been commissioned to create a statue in human form to rise over the sea at Dollymount. The work was withdrawn without explanation and a statue of the Blessed Virgin Mary erected in its stead, after which Eddie would have nothing more to do with the art establishment. Cussed to the last, he left a creative legacy that littered his house and garden, probably a warehouse or two, and a few select galleries belonging to people Eddie hadn't fallen out with.

Eddie's Dollymount sculpture was lit by a slanting sun. A tall, rough-hewn column of granite set in a clearing among the trees, it seemed at first sight to be just that. A block of granite with no discernible artistic merit. And maybe it was the angle of the sun – or maybe it was Hayden reading meaning into it that wasn't there – but it seemed to draw the viewer artfully in until it came to resemble, in a vaguely postmodern way, the imposing figure of an Irish icon: early twentieth century revolutionary and feminist Countess Constance Markievicz, standing austerely in the midst of Eddie's trees.

He'd loved those fruit trees as a boy. Clambering up the boughs for the highest sun-kissed apple. Collecting windfalls for Uncle Eddie's Sweet Ambrosia, an apple and pear cider that – but Hayden couldn't bear to think about it.

He wandered through the cluster of trees to the shed and peered in. Stacks of canvasses. An easel with a work-in-progress propped against it. Paint. Tins of turpentine. He retraced his steps to the back door and stood for a moment taking everything in, glancing once again at the statue. The sun had sunk behind the trees. The Countess had mysteriously fled. He turned and went inside.

Uncle Eddie's Sweet Ambrosia. Nectar of the gods, yes, but the hangover! And the blackouts! Never again. No more AA for Hayden. No more of his self-appointed minder, Trace. Luckily, he'd put the width of the Irish Sea between the two of them. No forwarding address. End of subject. He was finished with the drink. Full stop.

Until, that is, the door to the cellar caught his eye. It stood unobtrusively next to the kitchen cupboards and might have been mistaken for the entrance to a scullery. Hayden smiled ruefully. If he'd still been drinking he would have gone straight down there for a couple of bottles or, better still, a crate. Uncle Eddie cheering him on, or jeering at him, depending on the old sod's mood. Who knows, he might even have joined in the revelry.

Funny thing, though. Hayden had been scared of the steep steps down into the dark as a child. He shuddered at the thought and returned to the present, but the memory had sparked something. A quick look, he thought. Strictly nostalgia. No harm in that.

He approached the door tentatively. It opened with a sharp, grating rasp onto a darkness beyond darkness. He felt for the light switch. Click. Typical Eddie. The cellar was bathed in a blood-red glow. A child gate with a small plaque on it blocked his way. He bent down to read it. *Artist Descending into Hades.* An obvious reference to the ladder leading down into the cellar's Stygian depths. Hayden unlatched the gate and stepped gingerly onto – Jesus! He nearly stepped onto nothing. Was this Eddie's idea of a joke? Was he trying to kill someone?

Hayden's eyes slowly accustomed to the gloomy red light. Interesting. The ladder had twisted onto its side. But why? Hayden had been to Tate Modern – twice – so he knew his modern art. Perhaps Eddie was suggesting...

No. It didn't make sense. Everything Eddie did was a work of art, but this was a cellar. He must have intended the ladder for practical use as well.

Hayden examined the doorway. The ladder had been fixed at both sides with bolts, but one of the uprights had snapped. He bent down for a closer examination. Odd. It hadn't simply cracked. It had been cut with a saw, but not all the way through. Why would Eddie do that? Surely if he was removing the ladder, he'd just undo the bolts securing it to the doorjamb. Maybe it was an artistic statement?

Hayden's head hurt.

He'd only been to Tate Modern twice.

7

He was still mulling this over the following morning as he sat in the garden, his bag packed, waiting for Bram to pick him up to take him to the airport. Long hot summer. Triple rent. Rich. Foetus. AA Trace. Gravesend. Set all that against the delights of Clontarf on a beautiful balmy day. Perfect for this leafiest and loveliest of suburbs. London, on the other hand? Stifling at this time of year. Sweltering heat, fume-belching cars, and oh, for the smell of the sea! Could be a line from a poem there. Yeats? My thought, by the way, not Hayden's. Possibly brought on by the fact that Eddie's statue, angled by the glorious morning sun, bore an uncanny resemblance to a youthful Maud Gonne.

Hayden's thoughts were more prosaic as he went back inside and grabbed his bag. Bram wouldn't be late. He knew this. Bram's previous reference to timekeeping was based on a lazy stereotype of public transport. Bus driver humour. Hayden smiled wryly as he crunched down the gravel path. *Here's one you can use.*

He spotted the three aunts in their front garden peering at him over the top of the cotoneaster. One cotoneaster, three heads. He strolled over.

'Howaya, Hayding.'

'We were just pruning the roses. Seen you over the top.'

'Talking to yourself. So, how's tings?'

'I'm off back to London,' he said.

They seemed, for some reason, cheered by this news. Odd response. They were very fond of Hayden, so why would they want him to leave? Did they, perhaps, know something he didn't? At any rate, they brightened visibly for a brief moment, then went back to the social niceties.

'Aww, Hayding. So soon?'

'But you've hardly *been* here.'

'You'll be sorely missed, dough. Won't he, ladies?'

'Oh, undoubtably.'

'I did tell you I was just here for the funeral,' said Hayden. He hadn't.

'Well bong voyage. We'll let you know about the will.'

'You never know. Your luck might be in.'

'I doubt it,' said Hayden. He knew Eddie.

'So do we, Hayding,' said the three aunts.

'Anyway, say hello to your mammy and daddy.'

'My parents,' said Hayden, 'are in Waikiki.' His tone was measured, bordering on curt.

'Waikiki? Isn't that lovely? I'll tell you someting. *We* could do wit a hollyer, couldn't we, girls?'

'It's not a holiday,' said Hayden. 'They live there.'

The three aunts knew that already. Hayden's tone segued from curt to hurt. 'I haven't seen them since the day before my seventh birthday.'

They knew that already too, but all three sighed deeply as Bram pulled up and got out of the car.

'Ah well. That's the modering world for you, Hayding.'

They turned, three heads as one, to Bram.

'Anyway, that'll be your lift. Howaya, Abe. Did someone steal your bus?'

'Nice one, ladies,' said Bram. He punched Hayden on the shoulder. 'You can use that.'

Hayden said nothing. He kissed his three aunts on the tops of their dear little heads, pointed out that they were pruning the cotoneaster, not the roses, and left them to it. He tossed his overnight bag on the back seat and strapped himself in. Bram eased her into whatever it is you do with cars – I don't drive, myself – and they were off. As he drove along Kincora Road towards Castle Avenue, Bram pointed to a house on the left.

'See the brown plaque there?' he said.

'Erwin Schrödinger, 1887-1961,' groaned Hayden. He knew what was coming next.

'Good man yourself,' said Bram. 'Well done.'

Hayden let it pass. He was brought up here. Erwin Schrödinger, of Schrödinger's Cat fame, lived there after the war. He knew this already. Thank you, Bram. But Bram wasn't finished yet. He never was.

'Funny thing about your man,' he said. 'Whatever about that experiment of his, the same cat would be long dead by now one way or the other.' He punched Hayden playfully on the shoulder. 'I'm just thinking of the implications for quantum mechanics.'

This was exactly the same witticism Bram had used last time they'd passed the plaque. Fair enough, Bram liked to show off his sense of humour. But you can't just repeat the same gag every time you pass the same bloody landmark. Hayden had to call him on it.

'Jesus, Bram,' he said. 'You told exactly the same story last time.'

'Glad you noticed,' said Bram. 'I learned from the master.'

'Sorry?'

Bram chuckled. 'Come on, Haydo,' he said. 'I've seen your act now – how many times?'

'And? What's that got to do with it?'

'What, you spend every weekend in Scrabster?' He chuckled again. 'See where I'm going with this?'

Oldest, best and most infuriating friend. Bram drove on.

'Gas girls, the aunts,' he said. 'Thing is, though. I know something they don't.' He chuckled at the thought.

Hayden sighed inwardly. Another hilarious Bramecdote. Best get it over with. 'What do you know that they don't?' he asked as they approached the Howth Road intersection.

Bram seemed relieved. 'Glad you asked me that.' He whipped his mobile out. 'I took another shot of Eddie in his coffin.' Hayden grabbed the mobile from Bram as an acceptable alternative to crashing, and examined the screen. Eddie lay dead in his coffin in the background. Bram, in the foreground, gave the thumbs up.

'Lucky the old dears didn't see *that* one,' chortled Bram.

Hayden looked closer. 'What's that on his forehead?'

'You mean the gash?' said Bram. 'It's a gash. How's the novel coming along?'

'How did he get that?'

Bram thought about it. 'Syphilis?'

Hayden said nothing. A deep gash on the forehead and no-one had seen fit to mention it? A ladder to the cellar sawn almost fully through and tilted onto its side? Perhaps it wasn't modern art at all. Perhaps it was –

'Thing is,' said Bram, 'I've been giving a bit of thought to your book. Can't write 'em myself, dunno why, but other people's stuff? It's all up here,' – he tapped his forehead – 'so how's about you run your ideas past me and we'll see what I come up with? Might be a help, might not.'

Hayden sat in silence for some time as the car approached the turnoff to the airport. Bram was halfway around the roundabout when Hayden spoke.

'Turn the car back,' he said. 'I think Eddie's been murdered.'

'Inciting incident,' said Bram. 'Excellent. I'll give it some thought.'

And he drove straight on.

8

It's always difficult for someone like Bram to separate fact
from fiction. Eddie murdered? Too much for him to take in.
No point pushing it, so Hayden eventually settled for saying he
wanted to spend a bit more time on the home patch. Soak up
the atmosphere. Bram worked this through in his mind as they
turned back into Kincora Road.

'You've decided to set it in Clontarf,' he said. 'Good move.
Possible title: *Clean Streets*. You know. As in –'

'I know, Bram,' said Hayden. 'I know.'

Bram had just slowed down for a speed bump when – *wow*!
Professor Emeritus Larry Stern cycled past, his shock of white
hair flapping furiously in the bike-induced breeze. I mean,
serendipity or what? Professor Emeritus Larry Stern, Dept. of
Comedic Studies, CDU. Author of several seminal works on
this most complex of subjects. His masterpiece, *A Learned
Disquisition on the Theory and Practice of Comedy*, is never
far from my bedside table, or, indeed, my thoughts. His short
introduction to the subject, *Mirth: A User's Guide*, which posits
five levels of comedy, is highly recommended for the uninitiated.

Now, I don't want to get lost on a tangent, but I wish I
could have followed the professor. As I've become familiar with
his impressive body of work over the years, I've found myself
referring to him as one would to a philosopher; as a guide,
if you will, through the seemingly endless complexities of this
Sturm und Drang we call life. Perhaps he was running a summer
course at City of Dublin University. If so, I desperately wanted
to join.

I filed the professor away for future reference as Bram pulled the car to a halt outside Eddie's.

Hayden hopped out. The three aunts waved from behind the cotoneaster.

'Howaya, stranger. Coo-ee.'

'Seems like only twenty minutes since you were last here.'

'That'll be the oul dementia kicking in.'

'No, it won't,' said Hayden, crossing the road. 'I *was* here twenty minutes ago.'

'Did you forget someting? Did you?'

'Only that could be early onset.'

'We'd see a doctor quick if we were you, Hayding.'

'Before you forget.'

Hayden decided to get to the point. 'The gash on Eddie's forehead,' he said. 'Thoughts?'

His words had a surprising effect. His aunts seemed to shrivel into the bush like a three-headed tortoise. Hayden waited. They reappeared.

'That's an ingrown birtmark, Hayding. They grow out when you're dead.'

'Or syphilis.'

'That's what *I* said,' said Bram, getting out of the car.

'Oh, did you now? Well *we* were joking, weren't we girls?

'A bit of respect for the dead *if it's all the same to you.*'

'But we'd go for ingrown birtmark, Hayding. They only manifest themselves post mortem, don't they, ladies?'

'That's Latin, Hayding. But you'll undoubtably know that from your classical education wit the Christian Brothers in Fairview.'

'The point is,' said Hayden pointedly, 'I've decided to stick around for a while.' He was about to say 'Something about this whole business stinks', but you never knew what convoluted byroads of the English language the three aunts would go down with that one. 'I need a bit of a break,' he said instead.

'From what, Hayding?'

'More to the point, *for* what?'

'To what exalted purpose, if any, do you deign to grace us wit your estimable presence?'

'In a word.'

Hayden regretted his response as soon as it popped out. 'I'm writing a novel, actually.'

'Oh now. Excusez-nous.'

'Will we be in it, Hayding? Will we?'

'Not as such,' he replied. 'It's not that kind of novel.'

Then, before they could set off babbling again, he thanked Bram, waved to his dearly beloved aunts, strode briskly back across the road and crunched up the drive to Eddie's. Bram returned to his car and drove gratefully off. The three aunts resumed pruning and said nothing, each lost in her own deep thoughts, and all three lost in each other's.

'Turn the car back. I think Eddie's been murdered.' Hayden might just as easily have said 'Turn the car back. I need a bit of a break,' because that's exactly what he needed – and where better than his late uncle's house in leafy Clontarf?

Hayden, though, didn't see it as a break. No, Hayden was a man with a mission. He dumped his bag on the sofa, marched back out the front door and went around the side of the house. An old, black bicycle lay against the wall. Behind it, a rusty ladder. He moved the bike and laid it to rest against the privet. He then hoicked the ladder over his shoulder and made his way, with difficulty, to the front door. Put the ladder down first, then open the door. Makes sense when you think about it, but it's not what Hayden did. I was reminded of a scene from an old 1912 black-and-white two-reeler, *Apoplexy*, in which the heavily moustachioed silent screen icon Finlay Jameson fails to get a ladder past the front door and ends up demolishing the doorframe, the building, and, thanks to the house of cards effect, the whole street, 'with hilarious consequences'.[1] Wonderful comedian, Jameson. Even his moustache had funny bones. Not to mention his heavily-insured skipping rope eyebrows. My own particular favourite *Furious Finlay* short has him pushing a gorilla over a rickety bridge, only to meet a self-propelled piano coming the other way.

But this is by the by. Hayden eventually manoeuvred the ladder inside the house and lowered it into the cellar. Extended to its double length, it thumped satisfyingly onto the floor below. He switched the light on, stepped gingerly onto the top rung, and started the steep descent at the point where the original ladder had snapped. He stopped. There was no doubt about it. A saw had been applied to the left-hand upright. It had been sawn most of the way through. He ran his fingers along the edge to where it had snapped. His mind racing now, he continued his descent. The floor underfoot was tightly packed earth and, as he became accustomed to the light, he almost tripped on an overturned wooden drink crate. He set it face up.

He was about to move on when the light reflected off something in one of the empty bottle compartments. He reached down and prised it out. A pair of broken spectacles! Eddie's. He delicately disentangled the twisted wire of the frame. Bloodstained. As, he now saw, was the edge of the crate. Could this explain the large gash on Eddie's forehead? Had he been descending the ladder, possibly to replenish his supply of Sweet Ambrosia, then fallen, probably drunk, to the wooden crate beneath? But the ladder was sawn through. Why had no-one seen fit to investigate Eddie's death? To suspect foul play? He glanced quickly around the cellar. Silence and shadows. Cobwebs and canvases. He climbed back up and out into the daylight.

This was serious.

It wasn't crime fiction.

It was fact.

[1] Prof. Larry Stern, *Disquisition*, Chapter XIV – *Other People's Misery.*

The sun shone in an azure blue sky. I borrowed that line from an essay I wrote when I was nine. Azure. Blue. Same thing. I didn't know that then, I do now. We live and learn.

As Hayden emerged from the darkness of the cellar into the light, I suddenly had the urge to go to Dollymount for a swim, but that's the trouble with murder; you've got to follow the corpse. And this, as far as Hayden was concerned, was beginning to look premeditated. Which begged the question: how do you solve a homicide? In the real world, the short answer is you don't. You go to the Gardaí. That's their job. While they're solving it, you write a crime novel. That's *your* job.

The local Garda station being a fair old walk from Eddie's, Hayden decided the bike might be a good idea. It was a bit rusty and in need of a good oiling but – interesting this – no need to pump the tyres, even though it clearly hadn't been used for quite some time, judging by the rust. Not that Hayden noticed, but I did.

Hayden wheeled it down Eddie's drive and hopped on. It took him seven minutes to creak noisily from Eddie's to the station and park the bike on the steps. Surely no-one would think of nicking it there? The simple answer to that question is: yes, they would. The reason they didn't was because it was a rusty old contraption with a small family of spiders underneath the saddle.

Hayden loped up the steps, out of the sunlight and over to reception. Some time later, he was ushered into a small room on the first floor. Chairs. Table. Dusty blinds. A bluebottle in search of a window. Behind the table, on a tilted chair with one prodigious boot resting on the table, a toothpick in his mouth, lounged Detective Inspector Lou Brannigan. I could describe him in detail, but I don't think I need to. The boot on the desk, not to mention the casual poke of the toothpick, says it all. As does the trilby perched on the back of his head. Now, a trilby can be either trendy or naff; it all depends who's wearing it. When Brannigan looked at himself he saw trendy. Everyone else saw naff.

He motioned to a seat with the toothpick.

'So,' he said when Hayden had been seated for several minutes, 'you breeze in here and tell the lad out front your Uncle Eddie owes his untimely demise at the age of, what – eighty-six? – to the involvement of a third party. Now how do you suppose we missed that?'

'I have no idea,' said Hayden. He was lying. He had several ideas, none of them reflecting favourably on the guards.

Lou Brannigan extracted a small portion of fatty bacon from his molars and wiped the toothpick on his trouser leg. 'I'll tell you what,' he said. 'Man to man. Let you bring the Garda Síochána, as represented by myself, up to speed on this allegedly heinous crime.'

'Well –' said Hayden.

Lou Brannigan raised his toothpick for silence.

'Before you start,' he said. 'They tell me you're a comeejin. You might like to leaven your account with a few bon mots, witty asides and mebbe the odd jokeroony. It's a fierce hot afternoon and my sleep was interrupted yet again last night' – he sighed, rearranging his boots with great deliberation – 'by the increasing levels of criminality on this tragic little isle of ours in times of undoubted flux.' He leaned further back in his chair and returned the toothpick to his mouth. 'You have the floor.'

Hayden, glad to unburden himself, told Lou Brannigan everything. The phone call on stage. The trip back. The funeral. The scar. The twisted metal of the cellar steps and finally, the bloodied crate and broken glasses. I say finally. He couldn't help but mention that he'd decided to stay for a few days.

'I'm writing a novel, actually,' he said, the word 'actually' out of his mouth before he could stop it.

'Do you tell me so?' said Brannigan. 'And what, precisely, is its import? What is it about?'

'Early days,' said Hayden, 'but it's a murder mystery.'

'Well now,' said Brannigan, 'and you must be the fierce brainy gent. I'm an avid reader of the murder mystery genre myself. Takes my mind off the job, d'ye see. *Holy Joe*, now, there's a book. That'd be my own particular favourite by a Limerick mile.' He patted his stomach affectionately and sighed. 'Of course, it's his ould mammy I feel for. Holy Joe indeed, for he treated her very badly. Very badly indeed.' He seemed lost, for a moment, elsewhere. Then he returned, genially, to base. He added a second boot to the table. 'Now re this deceased relative of yours,' he said, 'do you think we have the man or, indeed, given the equal opportunities world we inhabit these days, lady-power to investigate every poxy little alleged murder? And anyway, you seem to know more about it than I do. Why not put in a bit of legwork and solve it yourself?' He placed one boot on top of the other and thought about switching teeth with the pick. 'Sure amn't I run off my feet here. We simply don't have the resources.' He flicked his toothpick at the waste bin. 'Answer me this. I believe the aforementioned Uncle Eddie, hereinafter referred to as "the murderee" is, to coin a cliché, not only dead but also buried.'

'Cremated,' said Hayden.

Brannigan chortled silently. 'Cremated, is it? So, let's get this straight. You want us to exhume the feckin ashes, hoh? Listen, if it was murder itself and it happened here or hereabouts, our very own Frankie Pope is assuredly your man. We've been trying to get something on that boyo for yonks. Unsuccessfully thus far, I might add. And I wouldn't mind, but he's holed up in solitary splendour not half a mile from this very room. Hiding in plain sight, if you follow my gist.' He sighed wearily with the weight of his knowledge. 'Frankie, aka Francis, is only the youngest, slipperiest member of the toughest, meanest, orneriest family in Dublin. The brains behind the outfit. The man who's never there.'

Hayden was still confused. 'Orneriest?'

'That's what I said, bud. You got a problem with that?'

'No, no. Just – good word.'

'Frankie Pope and his band of half-wit brothers. If the venerable Eddie has indeed been helped on his way to the Big D, that'd be my educated guess.' Brannigan redistributed his bulk with a loud grunt. 'Sadly for both of us, however,' he continued, 'I can't sit around here all day indulging in tittle tattle and hearsay. Not to mention any crackpot theory that walks through that door.' He slid a sheet of paper across the desk. 'Could I maybe get you to fill out this evaluation sheet at the desk beyond? Level of satisfaction with service provided. Male stroke female stroke other, delete as appropriate. Caucasian stroke person of colour stroke other, ditto. Oh, and with reference to your tome. If you're looking for a flawed anti-hero with an interesting past...'

He left the rest of the sentence floating on the stale, dusty air.

Hayden took the evaluation sheet and turned back at the door. 'So where exactly does this Frankie Pope character live?'

Brannigan extracted a replacement toothpick from a small container and chortled affably. 'Oh now,' he said. 'You want *me* to do all the work?'

Hayden asked at reception. Frankie Pope lived in so-called 'solitary splendour' in a big, detached, redbrick house on Seafield Road. From the description, Hayden recognised it as the house immediately backing onto Eddie's, the one he could see from the garden. Handy on one level, but very intimidating if you knew who owned it, because Frankie Pope sounded pretty nasty. He knew the sort, though not in real life. Cold, manipulative psychopaths, with a whole family of lesser psychopaths to do their evil bidding. Hayden experienced a momentary quiver of fear as he cycled up Haddon Road on the return trip, but then his rational mind took over. Why would Frankie Pope go to all the trouble of sawing through Eddie's cellar steps when he could have him wasted with a drive-by shooting, no questions asked? This was just lazy thinking on Lou Brannigan's part. He might rearrange his boots on the table or flick another toothpick at the bin – the first one missed, by the way – but that's as far as his detective skills seemed to go.

A quick interjection, if I may, for purposes of clarification. The Lou Brannigan as presented up to this point is not typical of the many decent, hard-working men and women who swell the ranks of the Gardaí. I'm covering my back here. A longer, gushing and, some might say, craven appreciation of this fine body can be found in *The Annotated Sloot*.[2] Let's leave it there for now.

Hayden, by this stage, had gone inside. He stood gazing meditatively out of the window to the back garden. The sun was angled across the statue which bore, at precisely 18.27, an uncanny resemblance to Dorothy Stopford Price. Very impressive, but Hayden was distracted by his preparations for the task ahead. On a shelf he found an old teapot, a handmade cosy in the shape of a bishop's work hat – in World of Eddie, even a lowly teapot was a work of art – and a caddy half full of finest Assam. Rich. Robust. A muscular breakfast tea known for its malty flavour and, interestingly, in its small-leaf form, a staple of Irish Breakfast Tea. Hayden knew all this. A recent convert to abstinence and, as a direct consequence of same, to the pleasures of the four-minute brew.

Maybe Lou Brannigan was right. Maybe, just maybe, there was no foul play. Hayden abandoned the tea, opened the cellar door, put the light on and stared into the depths. The way the twisted ladder had settled, its offkilteredness, *was* pretty Tate

---

[2] 'Not quite the beach read I was led to expect' – *The Lady*

Modernesque. So how was this for a scenario? Eddie had created his *Artist Descending into Hades*. He wasn't happy. Rungs that work? Too conventional. He decided to reposition them. Started to sever the ladder with the aid of a saw and a glass of his homemade hooch. The job was almost done. He ran out of his tipple of choice, went to the cellar to get some more, forgot, in his cups, that he was in the middle of re-imagining his artwork, stepped on the top rung, snapped the ladder from its moorings and fell to his untimely death. Yes, that was probably it. Pretty simple when you worked it through. All you had to do was think yourself into the mind of an artist. Eddie's death was tragic but accidental. Case closed.

It made total sense, particularly if you wanted an easy life.

So where now for Hayden? He'd stay on in Clontarf, write in the mornings, enjoy his afternoons and evenings off. This suited him perfectly, and why wouldn't it? It also suited *me* perfectly. I could now pursue whatever course on the comedic arts Professor Stern was running, without the inconvenience of keeping an eye on the plot. Double perfect.

Or was it? If Eddie's death was really nothing but a tragic accident, why read on? I don't think I'm giving too much away to suggest that new information comes to light about Eddie – but Hayden doesn't know this yet, which puts you one step ahead of our reluctant detective.

Intrigued?

Trust me. I know what I'm doing.

Honest.

I've read all the books.

10

Hayden sat at Eddie's writing desk. It felt strange. Almost as if he was channelling something; except he didn't know what that something was. It made him think about why he was writing the novel in the first place. The need to get off the standup circle of hell? There was that. But there was also something else. He certainly didn't feel the need to impress his father. His father had never paid him any attention whatever he did, so a novel wasn't going to make a difference one way or the other. Not that it bothered him particularly. But Eddie's desk. It felt right, somehow, to be sitting there to start the novel, although he wasn't quite sure why.

Whatever about that, there was a mountain of clutter to sort out first, so he made a start. He binned a few unopened bills, an empty envelope for parish dues and a leaflet about recycling. Under the Everest of paper sat Eddie's answering machine, its red light blinking. One message. He left the remaining papers for now and was about to press play when, well, he didn't. The message wasn't going anywhere and besides, he had a novel to write. He'd listen to it later. Good call, Hayden. Time to get stuck in. It sounds, on the face of it, like a pretty no-nonsense approach. Sign of a real pro.

Theoretically.

Over the next couple of hours, he sharpened his metaphorical pencils. Moved his desk to get a better view. Moved it back. Typical writerly activity. He was still faced with the same blank page, though, so he tore it out and concentrated his attention on a replacement, also blank. It was a short step from this to staring out the window at the statue's ever-changing face and reading the blurbs on the backs of other people's books. He'd made a mistake placing Bram's charity shop box under the desk, because some time later, and he couldn't figure out how or when it had happened, his own work had been set aside and he was twenty pages into a crime noir set in 1950's San Francisco: *Two in a Bed*, by Gay McQueen. S&M-friendly pulp. Brad finds the S, not to mention the M, quite pleasant, but when Clint shaves off the sleeping Brad's mustache [*sic*] in a fit of pique...

Not a great book, but once you start reading these things you can't put 'em down. By the time he'd finished, it was early evening. He managed to scrape together the makings of a modest meal; to be precise, a tin of sardines, the remains of a packet of oatcakes and a small bowl of soggy crisps from the wake. As he sat eating, his eye fell on Eddie's tapes.

The tapes were neatly arranged, as they had been since Hayden was a child, on a set of mahogany shelves above Eddie's desk. Each shelf was packed tight with slim cardboard containers. As a child, even as a young man, Eddie had forbidden him to touch them, never mind open the dusty boxes. This, he was told, was work. Just Eddie, an antiquated recorder, and a very occasional guest. But Eddie was gone now, so Hayden put his plate down and, almost gleeful at the wilful transgression, prised one of the boxes out. He opened it and removed its contents. A reel-to-reel tape, named and dated. Hayden put it back and slid another from its box. Same thing. Eddie had amassed an impressive collection. Hayden ran his eye along the neatly hand-printed labels, all arranged chronologically.

- *Eddie At Work XXI*
- *Eddie At Play III*
- *Monologues*
- *Sam*
- *More Sam*

And so on. Fascinating stuff. Hayden took the earliest one out. *Eddie at Work I*. It was dated *March '51*.

The recorder still sat on the old oak table in the corner, complete with a large pair of dark brown, leather-encased headphones. He had no idea how to operate it. Eddie had declared it a no-go area, and you didn't cross Eddie. In the lid-flap, however, he found a dog-eared user's manual, so he set about working out how to attach the tape from one spool to the other. It turned out to be quite a meditative process, a bit like, well, meditation, and Hayden's whole being was suffused with a gentle wellness as he became attuned to the slower rhythms of yesteryear.

He removed the tape from its sleeve, clicked it onto the recorder, wound it through and attached it to the feeder tape. He inserted the headphones, turned the lever on and settled back into the old mahogany swivel chair worn smooth by decades of Eddie.

I have no intention of giving a verbatim transcription of what might be called *The Eddie Tapes.* That would be a book in itself.[3] Fascinating stuff, though – an alternative version of Ireland from the mid- to late-twentieth century – and Hayden was riveted from the off. Eddie on Eddie. Eddie on his working methods. Eddie in conversation. A kind of aural logbook charting his creative development. The first tape worked through and started spinning wildly as it reached the end of the spool. Hayden placed it carefully back in the box and returned it to its shelf. He chose another one at random. *Eddie at Work IV, June '53.* Eddie in his mid-twenties, and already he'd started experimenting with sound. He was now listening to tapes of himself 'as a younger man', commenting playfully on the passage of time by conversing with his earlier self. A mixture of morbid, absurd and hilarious. 'Two weeks older,' he intones at one point, 'two weeks closer to the grave. Ah-h-h, the grave.' He must have been all of twenty-five at the time.

---

[3] It *is* a book in itself: *The Annotated Sloot: Vol XII.*

Hayden was hooked. But as he chose another tape at random, Eddie in conversation with the downright morose *Sam*, he began to feel unsettled. What was he doing in this house filled with memories, childhood, and Eddie?

He yawned and stretched. Time for bed. He'd just put the lights out and was about to settle down on the sofa when he remembered the message on the answering machine. He padded across the room in his underpants and pressed Play. 'You have one message. Message received Tuesday May 31st.'

The date was interesting. Just before Eddie died. He waited. A husky female voice: 'You haven't settled up yet, Eddie. So call Marina. I really must insist.' A short pause. The voice dropped a register. 'Or else, my sweet. Or else.'

End of message. Who was Marina? What hadn't Eddie settled up? Hayden pressed save. He was about to head back to the sofa to decode the message – which might or might not have sounded menacing – when his eye was caught by a rogue light outside the window, flickering near the back wall. He peered into the surrounding darkness. The light seemed to be swaying between the fruit trees, moving slowly towards the house. Word would have got out about a single man dying. Empty house. Hayden's terror was almost tangible.

Solution? He'd put the living room light back on. Problem solved. The would-be-burglar would think, 'third party on the premises' and take his or her swag-bag elsewhere. He reached for the light. The torch beam changed direction. Hayden's hand hovered over the switch. The intruder wasn't headed for the house after all. The torch lit up the shed, a hand reached out, the shed door opened. The torch went in.

Hayden toyed with the idea of a direct confrontation but decided, on balance, against. He'd monitor developments instead, see if he could get a description, possibly capture the intruder on his mobile. Good plan. It took care of the abject terror factor. Now where had he put his phone? Equally important, did it need recharging? Bit late for that now. The shed door opened. A dark shape emerged, torch now off, closed the door and retraced its steps towards the back wall. It was also, he noted, clutching something bigger than itself. Flat. Rectangular. Unmistakably one of Eddie's paintings. The burglar reached the back wall, placed the painting on top with ease, and clambered over. Seconds later, the painting disappeared from view.

Hayden's curiosity trumped his terror. He unlocked the back door quietly. Alert to the slightest noise, he darted up the garden, between the fruit trees, until he reached the back wall. He pulled himself up and peered over. Darkness. Silence. He threw a leg up and hoicked himself onto the wall. Still no sound in the surrounding moonless night. He waited a few moments and was about to give up and go back when a light went on in the redbrick house, illuminating a spacious, high-ceilinged living room. He could now make out a gravel area in front of the window and a long, sloping lawn. Inside the room, a dark-clad figure placed the painting on the mantelpiece and stood back to survey it. Hayden leaned forward and squinted in an effort to do the same, but from this distance could only make out a few blurred shapes. The dark-clad figure remained just that.

Hayden was about to let himself down on the other side and work his way closer to the window when it hit him. This was Frankie Pope's garden! He'd have guard dogs. Beefy minders. The usual paraphernalia of the criminal classes. Whatever the painting was, he could keep it. End of subject.

Except that it linked Frankie Pope to Eddie.

And that in itself was chilling.

11

Hayden was in the middle of not writing. It was mid-morning. Mornings had been allotted to getting on with his novel. He'd been sitting in front of a blank page waiting for inspiration for some time. Nothing. He pushed his chair back and looked longingly at Bram's book box. If he dipped into one, just one, it might set him off. He knew this wouldn't work. He'd get sucked into someone else's plot and that would be that. Morning gone. Besides, he'd arranged to meet Bram at the Nautical Buoy at midday. Only ten minutes to go until he headed off, but if the previous ten minutes were anything to go by they could take hours.

Just one. Honest. Just the blurb on the back. A quick fix. The drug terminology wasn't lost on him. He was desperate. Anything, anything to take his mind off not writing. Well, not *anything*. Not alcohol. He knew where that led. No, just a quick blurb. Where was the harm in that? Good question. Nowhere. Ah, but that's where the harm lay. He recognised in his reasoning the inner voice of the addict, but who cared? The addict didn't, and neither did Hayden.

He was about to succumb to his inner demon and pounce on the box when Eddie's phone rang. He pounced on that instead, with pathetic gratitude. See? He wasn't an addict after all. He could take a blurb or leave it. Given a choice, he'd chosen the phone. He didn't recognise the number, but why would he? And who, again, cared? Hayden didn't, and the addict, because Hayden wasn't one, didn't exist.

'Yes?'

'Oh, hi. Trace here.'

A woman's voice. But Trace? Who was Trace?

'Trace,' he said. 'And you are?'

'Trace,' said Trace. 'You know. Trace? AA?' Hayden stood up, stunned. 'So, when will you be back?' He started rooting in Eddie's drawer. Possibly a nervous reaction. A bottle opener. He ignored it. 'Thing is,' said Trace, 'I'm worried about you, over there in Dublin with all that, you know, temptation and suchlike.'

Hayden spluttered in disbelief. A pair of bicycle clips. He took them out. 'You've no right to worry about me. You're not my mother.'

'Who left when you were seven years old, Hayden. Who moved to Waikiki with your dad and left you mum-less ever since. Do you maybe want to talk about this?'

'I wasn't seven,' snapped Hayden. 'It was the day before my seventh birthday. And no I bloody don't.'

'Well it could be the root of your problem, love.'

Hayden wasn't having this. 'Two points: one, I don't have a problem and two, I'm not your love.'

'Admitting we have a problem is the first –'

'Hold on. You're right. I do have a problem. Well spotted, *love.*'

'See? Self-knowledge is the first step. Do you want to share it?'

'Yes. I do. You. You're the problem.'

He pulled an old nutcracker from the drawer and fondled it distractedly.

'That's it,' said Trace. 'Blame the messenger, Hayden. It's an old trick, but trust me, it never works. I should know, because whatever hell you've been through, I can assure you I've been through it too.'

'Well, thanks for sharing that. How did you get this number? No, wait, don't tell me. The Higher Power moves in mysterious ways. Well you tell the Higher Power –'

'That's not nice, Hayden. Edward McGlynn? Dublin? It wasn't that difficult.'

He put the nutcracker back and spotted a pair of opera glasses half-buried in the clutter. He pulled them out and held them up to the light.

'Another thing. You seem to know a hell of a lot about my private life.'

'I've seen your act.'

Fair point. Waikiki. Good comedy name. That's the problem with confessional comedy. Sometimes the truth is funnier. But still.

'My parents are none of your business,' he said. 'There's no temptation. Or – or *suchlike*. Bye now.'

'But what about the Ten Point Plan?'

Hayden didn't hear that bit. His ears were too furious. He slammed the phone down and stood by the desk, fuming, clutching the opera glasses. He looked down at his hands, took a closer look at the opera glasses, and, possible displacement therapy this, the very fact of looking, of engaging ocularly with the glasses, calmed him down. His ears stopped burning. He turned the glasses over and was soon lost in the aesthetic pleasure of their operaglassesness. He'd never seen a pair before. He didn't know if Eddie liked opera, but in a funny sort of way you didn't have to. The glasses were a thing of beauty in themselves, and he was about to train them on the garden to see if there were any sopranos lurking in the bushes when he suddenly remembered. Bram. Nautical Buoy. Midday.

He placed the opera glasses gently on the desk and closed his blank notebook with gratitude. Courtesy of Trace, the final ten minutes of his self-imposed routine had flown by in seeming seconds. Not that he thanked her for it. The woman was certifiable, but she was in London and he was in Dublin, so no harm done. All thoughts of Trace forgotten, he stepped into the light of a lovely June morning. The three aunts observed him from behind the cotoneaster and kept their own counsel.

The Nautical Buoy, newly refurbished, sat facing Dublin Bay. The interior was bright and welcoming, with a smattering of customers dotting the bar stools and bistro tables. The lunchtime crowd hadn't quite made it in yet. No sign of Bram. Over in the corner, guitarist Voot O'Rooney improvised a jazzy little number about the dish of the day, *Mushroom, Tomayto and Sweet Potato Pie.* Not that it was on the menu, but that's jazz for you: rhythm is all.

Hayden sat at a vacant table. He hadn't been in for some years and the changes were dramatic. From traditional dark pub, no women, tipped cigarettes a sign of effeminacy, to bright, inclusive, family-friendly bar/bistro. A shaft of sunshine from the skylight illuminated the distinguished-looking man at the counter, fedora in hand, voice projecting as if to the back stalls.

'A large contusion to the left ventricle suggested foul play, but it turned out he was a keen hurler so he died, as it were, in the line of duty. The clue? He was on a GAA pitch at the time. Auchentoshan single malt an't please you, Declan. I like to start the day alphabetically. And while you're preparing this estimable libation I'm off for a quick puff, no offence to our gay brethren.'

'Right you are, Mr. Quilty,' said the barman. 'None taken, I'm sure.'

Quilty strode to the door as if all eyes were on him. Hayden's were. This was the fedora-wearing drunk Bram had referred to as 'your man' before Eddie's funeral. A criminal pathologist, judging by his little speech. Interesting. Could be very useful. The sun, angled from the skylight, seemed to follow him across the floor. After he'd made his exit through the swing doors, it settled back on the glass of single malt Declan placed on the counter in front of Quilty's stool.

Before the doors had stopped swinging, Bram came in. The sunlight stayed where it was. He spotted Hayden and sauntered over.

'Pint?'

Hayden drummed his fingers on the table. 'I don't drink.'

'Half?'

Hayden decided to sit this one out.

'Glass of wine?'

'I'll have a coffee, thanks,' said Hayden. 'Hold the liqueur.'

Bram nodded in understanding. 'Scrabster, right?' He placed the order, two coffees, brought them over and pulled out a chair. 'Just passed your man on the way in,' he said. 'I'll tell you one thing. This place is on the up and up.'

'Your man?' said Hayden. 'Ah yes. Quilty. Pathologist by the sound of it. Cause of death, that sort of thing. Could be useful.'

Bram gave him an odd look as he sat down. 'Are we in work mode here?' he said. 'Fair enough. How's it shaping up?'

Hayden didn't want to talk about the novel.

'Eddie,' he said. 'I think he may have been murdered. Which means somebody out there must have done it. And if so – who?'

'Work it is,' said Bram. 'Good start. Get your reader involved.'

Hayden settled back. Two old friends with nothing left in common, coffee in front of them, nothing to be done about it; so he filled Bram in on the story so far. The gash on Eddie's forehead, which Bram already knew about. The cellar. The sawn-through ladder. The guards. The late night incident with the intruder. He was about to mention the answerphone message when a mild-mannered little man at the next table leaned over.

'Excuse me,' he simpered. 'Is anyone using the salt?'

Hayden waved it away impatiently. And here's the curious thing. The man has asked the question. He's got his answer. He doesn't take the salt. Interesting. If Hayden had been narrating this thrilling opus himself, he wouldn't have included that seemingly insignificant detail. Why? He didn't notice it. I did. One-nil to third person narration.

Hayden had been in mid-flow, but the man had upset his rhythm and Bram used the slight pause to interject.

'Brilliant. Write what you know, am I right?' He nodded gravely. 'It also means you can set it in Clontarf. Clever.'

Hayden was about to lead him gently back to the real world, but Bram had other ideas.

'Okay. Now as previously discussed, your great crime writers plot the story backwards. You know who dunnit. You work back. Plant clues. Set up the murder. *Then* you write it. So, you know your perp –'

'No,' said Hayden. 'I *don't* know "my perp".' He shook his head. 'If I knew who perped it –'

'Fine,' said Bram. 'Keep yourself in the dark. That way you're as surprised as the reader. Equally valid. We don't know who dunnit. We don't know why he dunnit. Works either way.'

'Could be a she,' said Hayden.

'Blank sheet,' said Bram. 'I can live with that.'

Hayden sighed wearily. 'This is not a book, Bram. This is real life. Eddie is a real person and someone out there, also presumably real, may have killed him.'

But Bram didn't hear the last bit, because he was off again. 'Your sleuth,' he said. 'Let's call him –'

'Let's call him Hayden,' said Hayden.

Bram nodded. 'Fine, if it gets you started. You can change it later. He's a man alone. Bit of an outsider. Addicted to painkillers. Tragic past. Rescued a baby from a bomb in Baghdad. Beirut? Belfast? Lost his left leg and most of his upper torso when the second bomb went off. I don't think that's been done.' Hayden's heart sank. Confiding in Bram possibly wasn't such a good idea after all, but there seemed to be no stopping him. 'Then there's your talk-to person,' Bram continued. 'Also as previously mentioned.'

'I remember him well,' said Hayden. 'Someone a bit thick so you can explain stuff to the reader. Let's call him Bram.'

'The name isn't important at this stage,' said Bram. 'We'll think of something.' He rooted through his brain for other pearls of advice. 'Ah. Final point. The love interest. We're looking at a series here. Your sleuth has to walk away from the femme fatale. Tough one. Maybe *she* dunnit. But you take my point. He can't start book two with a couple of kids and a house in

Portmarnock.' Bram punched the table gently for effect. 'Dark past yes, mortgage no.'

Hayden was about to change the subject – prostate cancer, bus timetables, anything – when he remembered the answerphone message.

'By the way,' he said, 'you don't happen to know a woman name of Marina?'

Bram sat back in his seat. 'Not intimately,' he said. 'Wish I did though. Why?'

'I have to pay her a visit.'

'Do you now?' said Bram. 'And why would that be?'

'Oh, you know,' said Hayden, who didn't want to go back to the Eddie narrative. 'Business.'

'Business,' said Bram. 'Like that, is it?'

'What's that supposed to mean?' said Hayden.

Bram sighed. 'Okay,' he said. 'Fair enough. Marina's your one with the red coupé. Lives next to your aunts. Moved in about a month ago. Big sign outside advertising her wares. But you'll know about that already. To be honest, I didn't think you had a problem in that direction.'

'Sorry?' said Hayden. 'What direction?'

'Oh now. Says he to me.' Bram checked his watch. 'Got to head, compadre. The afternoon shift waits for no man.'

Just then the swing doors flew open and Quilty returned from his quick puff. No point trying to push Bram further, so Hayden changed tack.

'Before you go,' he said. 'I could use a copy of that Eddie shot. You know. The one with the gash.'

'I'll do better than that,' said Bram. He whipped his phone out. A few quick hand movements. 'Job done,' he said. 'Check your inbox. Anyway,' – he punched Hayden playfully on the shoulder – 'here's me bus.'

Hayden waited until he'd gone, then opened the attachment. You could just about make out Eddie's wound on the small screen. He'd appeal to Quilty's vanity. He looked the vain sort.

A quick perusal, if you would be so kind, and do let me replenish your glass. Ballachulish, is it? He was about to go over when Quilty picked his fedora off the bar and waved it flamboyantly in a half circle. 'That's me away,' he declaimed. 'Busy day, busy day.'

He drained his tumbler and swirled dramatically towards the exit. He flung the swing doors open and all but bowed from the waist. 'Allow me, ladies,' he announced to the room, and the three aunts scuttled in.

'Why tank you, kind sir.'

'Nice to see there's *some* gentlemen left.'

'And if you don't tink it's being too forward, you remind all tree of us of the great actor manager Sir Donald Wolfit in his heyday.'

'In Macbet.'

'A vain, vain man, but my God, he could certingly reach the stalls.'

'Positively stentorian.'

'A rare compliment, ladies. I well remember his one-man Othello at Borris-in-Ossory Parish Hall. His Desdemona? Quite, quite heartbreaking, and his lightning removal and reapplication of face paint during the dying scene was a lesson in stagecraft I will assuredly take with me to the grave. Adieu, gentle ladies. Adieu.'

Quilty waved them in and exited stage left. The three aunts scurried excitedly across the plush carpet.

'There you are, Hayding.'

'We're down for the cream tea brunch.'

'Bit risqué on the old ticker front at our age, but c'est la mort.'

This led to a fit of giggles, which suggested possible comic intent. Hayden held seats for them and made the usual flattering noises, but as he left he was struck by a disquieting thought: they didn't seem surprised to see him. Why? Were they there to check up on his movements? He also noted, although it didn't seem significant at the time, that the salt was still on the table.

12

Hayden stood outside Marina's house, the garden almost obscured by blowsy blooms. No red coupé in the driveway, meaning no Marina. Hayden glanced at the sign.

Marina : Court

That was as much as he could see; the rest was hidden by rhododendrons. He was about to lean over and brush the hanging branches aside when a scarlet convertible slowed down, though not much, and careered into the driveway. A stunningly attractive woman hopped out and fumbled for her front door key. She shot Hayden a quizzical glance, located the key and opened the porch door. Her mobile rang; she answered it and went inside. Hayden aborted Plan A, braced himself and followed her up the driveway. She turned to close the door and, spotting Hayden, flashed him a bewitching smile. Hayden experienced a certain *je ne sais quoi*. A quickening of the pulse? A vague stirring in the loins? I'm trying to be subtle about this, but she was even more stunning close up. He steadied himself. This was strictly business.

She lowered the mobile. 'You're a bit early,' she said, 'but do come in.'

Hayden was thrown. That seemed a bit... forward? On the other hand, he was there to confront her. The phone message to Eddie. '*Or else*'? She didn't look the threatening type, but you never knew.

'Upstairs, first on the right,' she said, waving him in with her free hand. 'With you in a tick.'

Hayden ran that back to see if he'd heard correctly. Upstairs on the right. With you in tick. That was pretty much it. Back on her mobile, she followed him into the hall. 'Nonsense. It's incontrovertibly the oldest profession.' Quick pause. 'Of *course* you can quote me on that. Anyway, got to go. Client.' She pocketed her mobile and closed the front door. 'Bloody media.'

Hayden stood motionless at the foot of the stairs, unsure what to do next. This was all getting a bit complicated, and the hallway didn't help. Traditional layout, unlike Eddie's, but graced with what appeared to be Frida Kahlo nudes. Subtly erotic and adding, under the circumstances, to Hayden's mounting unease.

'Thing is,' he said, 'I've just dropped in for a quick word.'

Marina sighed. 'Let's get one thing straight. There's nothing to be ashamed of. Besides, you're booked for a double session.' She flicked through her mobile. 'Here we are. Bit early as I say, but you're here now. So up you go.'

Hayden was about to protest again when he heard the sound of a key in the front door. It opened. Lou Brannigan looked at Hayden. Hayden looked at Lou Brannigan. This, to Hayden at least, was getting increasingly bizarre. Marina cut across the stunned silence before it had even begun.

'Glad you could come, Detective Inspector. Still no sign. I'll just go and double check. In the meantime,' she added mischievously, 'my client here won't do as he's told. What is it with some people that they need such persuasion?' She smiled in what Hayden took to be a seductive manner and disappeared through a door towards the back. Brannigan fingered his trilby sheepishly and avoided eye contact.

'You heard what the lady said,' he muttered, but his heart wasn't in it.

Hayden wasn't a client. *He* knew this, but Lou Brannigan didn't. Cue a farcical scenario of mistaken identity, dropped trousers and the hypocrisy of the Dublin middle classes if we choose to go down that particular route. But that's the job of the theatre. Besides, the dropped trouser routine doesn't work so well on the page.

Hayden was about to blow the whistle on the client bit when Marina's call interrupted from the back garden. 'Here puss puss puss puss puss, here pussy pussy. Here puss puss puss puss puss, here pussy.'

I'm about to make a comedy point here, as examined in exhaustive but not exhausting detail in Professor Stern's *Mirth*.[4] The term 'pussy' has different meanings for different people. It happens to be a staple of low comedy and, as such, has no place in this book. Or does it? *Sloot* aims for higher things, but context is all. 'Cat' would be preferable to 'pussy' – it avoids accusations of smut – but 'cat' is not a word you use when calling your cat. 'Pussy', however, is.

Point made, the back door closed and Marina re-entered. 'Not a sign of the poor thing,' she sighed. 'What am I to do, Detective Inspector? I mean, it's not as if it's the first time this has happened.' She turned to Hayden. 'Three cats have disappeared in four weeks. It doesn't make sense.'

Lou Brannigan shifted his feet uncomfortably, as though wishing he was somewhere else. His mobile rang in his pocket. He answered it gratefully.

'I'm on it.' He put the mobile away. 'Armed robbery in Coolock,' he said. 'All the hallmarks of a Pope job.' He opened the front door. 'Relax,' he said. 'I'm on the pussycat too.'

'Chances are it's the Popes,' said Hayden drily.

Brannigan eyed him closely. 'What makes you say that?'

'Call it a hunch,' said Hayden. 'Male intuition.'

Brannigan seemed to be working something out in his head. Was this so-called comeejin having a bit of fun at his expense? He filed the idea away for future reference and turned to Marina.

'We're up to our eyes at the station this week,' he said.

'And it's still only Tuesday,' said Hayden.

---

[4] Prof. Larry Stern, *Disquisition*, Chapter IV – *Titters and Tittering: The Unsubtle Art of Innuendo.*

Brannigan added this to the file. Duly noted. He'd have a private word later.

Marina looked startled. 'Tuesday? I thought it was Wednesday.' She turned to Hayden. 'I thought you were my new referral. So, what *are* you doing here?'

Lou Brannigan put his hat on. 'I'll leave your client to explain that one,' he smirked, and left.

'Well?' said Marina. 'I'm waiting.'

Hayden felt suddenly vulnerable. He didn't want to confront Marina about the answerphone message any more, or anything else for that matter. He just couldn't tell how she'd take it.

'I...' he faltered.

Marina held the front door open, her seductive smile back in place. 'Sorry to rush you out,' she said. 'If today is Tuesday, I have an important client at half past. Oh, and next time,' she said, 'phone for an appointment. I'm fully booked up at the moment, but I'm sure I can fit you in soon. Or maybe I could suggest someone else?'

Thanks for the offer, but no, she couldn't. Hayden stood on the driveway after she'd closed the door, his head a jumble of thoughts, but this is what they boiled down to: Marina ran 'the oldest profession' from her home. Eddie owed her money. Hayden was about to confront her. Lou Brannigan arrived. He was stunned to see Hayden there. So is she, let's say, an escort? Which would make Brannigan her client? No. He had his own key, so he must be, let's say, her pimp. Conclusion? She'd phoned Eddie for money due. No response. She'd got Brannigan on the case. Maybe *he* bumped Eddie off? It certainly seemed plausible.

But that was only part of the jumble. Hayden, in spite of himself, had felt a powerful attraction to Marina, but she was undoubtedly a –

'Coo-ee!'

The three aunts stared at him from behind the cotoneaster.

'We seen you going into our highly alluring next-door-neighbour's palatial abode, Hayding.'

'You could do a lot worse.'

'A lady of independent means, wit her own residence, is not to be sneezed at in these uncerting times.'

'Plus she'll never be out of work wit *her* particular skills.'

'Not many people know this, Hayding, but we have it on the highest autority – '

'– it's the oldest profession.'

All three giggled happily.

'Trute be known, Hayding, we dabble a bit ourselves.'

Hayden screamed inwardly – The horror! The horror! – before striding across the road and up Eddie's driveway, his thoughts back on Marina. How best to describe them? Smitten but confused is close enough. The *Marina : Court* sign. Court. Courtesan. French word. Sex as a commodity. The illusion of romance.

As Hayden reached Eddie's, a ministerial car pulled onto the grass verge outside Marina's house and a chauffeur in a peaked cap emerged. He walked around the car, opened the back door, and a small man with a pronounced nervous condition got out and twitched up her driveway. Marina's front door opened and she ushered him in. Hayden glowered at them for a moment from the doorway. Then he, too, went inside.

Verschiebung. Lovely German word meaning displacement, transfer, deferral, and one that describes perfectly how Hayden coped with the Marina problem. Hayden was smitten but in denial. A small man with a twitch was, probably at this very moment, bounding into the 'treatment room' to be pleasured by Marina. Was ever *Verschiebung* more needed?

As soon as he was safely inside Eddie's house, Hayden slipped the opera glasses into his pocket and grabbed a chair. He went out to the garden, strode assertively to the back wall, placed the chair against it, stepped up and, assertiveness departed, peeked tentatively over. This was Frankie Pope's house. Luckily for Hayden, though, there was no-one in sight. He took the opera glasses out and trained them on the house, adjusting them till they focused on the red brick. He moved them slowly along till he reached the living room window. The painting was still on the mantelpiece. He concentrated hard, but no – even with the opera glasses, he couldn't make out any detail. Perhaps it was *Verschiebung* again, as his insistence on displacing any thoughts he might have involving Marina seemed to send him too far in the opposite direction, but he became uncharacteristically fearless. All thoughts of Dobermen, stocky thugs, twitching clients and Marina were banished as he clambered over the wall and moved swiftly across the manicured lawn, past a solitary oak, until he reached the imposing house. The window ledge stood at about seven feet from ground level, so he had to hoist himself up by his fingertips.

Urrrrrrrnnnnnnngh. He kept this to himself as he tensed every muscle and strained every sinew, until his eyes were on a level with the window sill. One last silent grunt and he was there. He peered in and... *what a room*! Magnificent, spacious, high-ceilinged and, more to the point, empty, which allowed him to study the painting on the mantelpiece at his leisure. A woman. Tall. Arresting. Reminiscent of someone, but he couldn't think who. He was sure he'd seen her somewhere before. She was positioned beside a tall, expansive fireplace in a long, flowing dress, one hand on the mantelpiece. Hayden recognised the mantelpiece as the same one the painting was sitting on. Very nineteenth century. Odd, though. She occupied the position normally reserved for the Victorian lord of the manor. Also incongruous was the glass of brandy in her free hand, her broad shoulders, and the nine-inch Cuban cigar smouldering between her lips. He'd just worked out who she reminded him of – the imposing woman from the funeral! – when he heard voices coming around the side of the house, growing louder by the second.

Sheer terror concentrated his mind as the voices approached. He dropped lightly to the ground and darted towards the giant oak, which may have been placed there by a benevolent and all-knowing God several centuries beforehand for precisely this purpose. Or maybe not. The important thing is that it was there, and that Hayden managed to conceal himself behind it just as a group of men loped around the side of the house like a troupe of silverback gorillas in the mating season, one prodding another in the chest and spitting vitriol. Hayden couldn't make out what they were saying. He didn't want to. He wanted to get out of that garden, now, and nothing else. Bit like a female gorilla.

The men had just reached the garden table when one of them, about to sit, sensed something not quite right. He may have sniffed the air. Frightened female alert. Silence fell. Hayden was beyond alarmed. Frankie Pope was supposed to live alone. Was this a family visit? The notorious Pope brothers gathered to plan a job? There must have been at least a dozen of them. What if they loped across the lawn towards the tree? He peeked around the side of the mighty oak. Two of the men – squat, muscular, unnervingly alike – stared straight at him, impassive. Hayden thought for one stupefied moment. Then he braced himself, turned and raced frantically towards the wall. He scrambled up and glanced quickly behind him to see if they'd given chase, but they hadn't. No movement whatsoever. One of them, very slowly and menacingly, raised a clenched fist, smiled enigmatically, opened the fist, finger-pistolled him, blew smoke off an imaginary gun. They laughed. A chilling we-know-where-you-live laugh. Then they turned away and got back to their vicious squabble.

Hayden fell onto the lawn on Eddie's side of the wall, quaking, and trembled his way back to the house. Frankie Pope had stolen Eddie's painting. Why? He had no idea. And now it had drawn him into the Popes' violent orbit.

On the plus side, all thoughts of Marina had totally disappeared.

13

Hayden re-entered the house on the verge of a panic attack. He began talking to himself, discussing his own fear. 'Nothing has actually happened, but something is about to. This I know. I also know that the something will contain a level of violence I haven't experienced since my first day at secondary school.'[5] How did he know this? He didn't. It was the panic attack talking. But sometimes, just sometimes, a panic attack knows more than you do. The panic attack expected a visit from the Popes, and it expected that visit soon.

In moments of stress, the tea-making ritual is known to bring an equilibrium of sorts. He'd read that somewhere or other. Possibly a Japanese novel. He put the kettle on, tipped used tea leaves out of the infuser and washed the teapot, *Verschiebung*ly, with shaking hands. He'd just placed a cup and saucer on a tray, one tinkling rhythmically as it made contact with the other, when his mobile rang. Rich. He disliked his agent intensely, but on the plus side, the panic attack wasn't Rich's fault. And maybe, just maybe, it was time to go back to London, which at that moment seemed like a distant and much-loved memory, not to mention an unsullied haven of peace. Might be an idea to see what Rich had to offer. Panic attack temporarily over, he accepted the call.

'Ay.'

'Dickie.'

[5] School motto: 'Give me a boy till he's seventeen, I will give you the fruitcake.'

'Rich, Ay. Rich.' Hayden relaxed. For the first time, it felt good to hear the sound of his agent's voice. 'September tour, Ay.' Hayden perked up. This felt better still. 'You'll be supporting –'

Back to worse. Hayden had a position. He didn't do support on out-of-town gigs. London was different. You went on early, you rushed off to another gig. No pecking order. Out of town was different. Rich knew that.

'Whoa, Rich. I don't do support.'

'Spare me, Ay. Thing is, you've been usurped, mate. It's your generational tectonic-plate-shift type thing. You with support? For 'with', read 'as'. That's the bad news.'

'And the good news?'

'Same line-up. You. Foetus O'Flaherty. In that order.'

Hayden was about to tell Rich exactly what he thought of the tectonic-plate-shift theory of comedy when a loud rap on the front door took his mind off this latest blow to his manhood. He'd been expecting the visit, felt he knew who it was and decided, as a result, to pop out the back way. Pretend he was pruning the statue. That way he might live to make his own dinner.

'Interesting offer, Rich,' he said. 'Got to go, though. I'm just off to stick a pin in your effigy.'

He opened the back door as the kettle entered the penultimate stage of the boiling process, the one where the noise shifts up a gear but the bubbling has yet to start. Two squat men stood blocking his way. He recognised them from the garden. Shaved heads. Tight-fitting suits. Bit like body doubles for each other. They smiled in unison.

'Psychic or fucken wha?'

The accent was hard. Guttural. Decidedly not Clontarf. Hayden fought the desire to soil himself.

'The Pope Twins. Jus so ya know.'

A second knock on the front door. The more identical of the twins brushed past Hayden and went to answer it. 'You can't be too careful these days,' he said. 'Could be annyone.'

His brother in crime pointed at his retreating back. 'JP,' he said. He pointed at himself. 'Benny. Mind if we come in? Good man.'

Probably a rhetorical question, as they were already in. Hayden bowed to the inevitable and closed the back door. His mouth was dry. So were his trousers. He was doing well, all things considered.

'Nice place, Clontarf,' said Benny. 'Wha's the fucken word? Genteel. Me an JP, we like a bih a genteel. Wha's this?'

He pointed at the teapot. Hayden located some saliva.

'It's a teapot. I was making a pot of tea when you –'

'Poh a tea. Nice. Haven't seen one a those in – well, *evah*. Very – wha's the word?'

'Genteel?' said Hayden.

'Rhetorical question,' said Benny. 'I was abouh to answer it meself. But yeh. Very genteel. An there's the kettle biled. Away you go, sonny.'

Hayden bridled at the 'sonny' bit; he was old enough to be Benny's uncle. But he said nothing. He scooped three heaped tea-spoonfuls of Assam into the infuser and poured boiling water over it and, because his hand was shaking, over the worktop. Closely watched by Benny.

'Always a pleasure watchin an artist ah work,' he said. 'No need for the cup. I'll explain when JP gehs back. Hold ih. Serendipiddy alert. Here comes the very man now.'

JP ambled in. 'Couple a Jehovah's Wihnesses. Now thass whah I call timin. I told em there was a man here abouh to meeh his maykah. They were del-*eerious*. Asked me to pass this on.' He held up a copy of the Holy Bible. 'Wha's wih the tea?'

'He was makin ih,' said Benny, 'So I said on you go.'

'Magic,' said JP. 'Any biccies?'

'I thought we weren' stoppin,' said Benny. 'Anyway, don't ya have to leh the fuckah brew?'

'Six minutes,' lied Hayden.

'Six fucken minutes? Live an learn, hoh? How long left?'

'Five minutes fifty seconds,' said Hayden. Another lie. It was more like four twenty.

'Five fifty?' said Benny. 'We'll be well gone by then. Thah righ, JP?'

'Spor on. Okay. Grab a seah. Leh's do this.'

He gave Eddie's writing seat a little twirl and motioned Hayden to sit. He sat. The Twins looked down on him almost, you'd be forgiven for thinking, benevolently. Benny's eye shifted to the table. 'Wha's wih the nohebewke?' he said.

Hayden couldn't help himself. 'I'm writing a novel,' he said.

The twins looked impressed.

'Brillo,' said JP without irony. 'Wha's it abouh?'

'Early days yet,' said Hayden, relaxing slightly into his favourite subject. 'It's – it's a crime novel, actually.'

'Go on then. Show us a bih.'

Hayden shifted uneasily. 'It's still fermenting.'

'Like the tea, hoh?'

'Sort of.'

'So, like, how long to go?'

Hayden looked at his watch. 'Just over five minutes,' he lied.

'I think he meant the bewke,' said Benny.

'Oh, that,' said Hayden. 'It sort of all depends on the fermenting process.'

JP coughed politely. 'Can *we* be in ih, like?'

Benny grabbed the chair excitedly. 'On'y here's the twist. We're the good guys. Cos we're noh in real life. Wish we were though.'

JP smirked happily. 'No we fucken don't.'

'On'y joshin,' said Benny. 'Anothah thing. You know scenes like this. Two baddies, one poor fuck in a chair. How comes the two baddies geh the best lines?'

'Yor righ there, Benny,' said JP. He looked at Hayden. 'Thoughts?'

Hayden thought. Quickly. As if his life depended on it. 'Maybe,' he said, 'the victim has other things on his mind.'

'Could be,' said JP, thoughtfully. 'Could be. Hadn' thought a thah. See? Thass why you're a wriher an we're noh.'

'Each to his own area of expertise,' said Benny, a line which would have suited a more relaxed Hayden very well. But he felt, on balance, that he might be better advised to go down the good listener route, which gave JP the floor.

'Speakin a which,' he said, leaning in till his nose almost touched Hayden's. 'Frankie's garden. You seen nuhhin, righ? Wha did ya see?'

'I saw nothing.'

Silence.

'Leh's try that again,' said JP. 'You seen nuhhin, righ? Wha did ya see?'

Hayden was confused.

'Nothing,' he said. 'I saw nothing.'

'Yor noh listenin,' said JP.

'Oh, right,' said Hayden. 'I seen nuhhin.'

'Good man,' said Benny. 'Thing is, we're proud a the vanacular. The homogenisation a local dialectics: thorny subject. How's thah tea comin on?'

'Oh,' said Hayden, 'not long now. Maybe, what, five minutes?'

'Care to reword thah? On'y when I first mentioned ih, the clock said *six* past. Ih now says *twelve* past. Higher Mahs not yor strong suhe?'

'It's – it's about ready now,' said Hayden.

'Excellen-fucken-teeho,' said Benny. 'A Plus. Top a the class.'

JP lifted the pot off the tray.

'So where would you like ih? In the mouh or poured over yor bollix?'

Hayden looked at him, unable or unwilling to formulate an answer. JP paused. A menacing pause. He held it for a long, meaningful moment. Then he put the pot back on the tray and turned to Benny.

'He seen nuhhin,' he said, sauntering towards the door.

And Benny sauntered in his wake.

As Hayden watched the Pope Twins leave from the window, strolling in the opposite direction came Detective Inspector Lou Brannigan. They exchanged barbed pleasantries as they passed, without easing the pace. Brannigan paused at Eddie's gate, glanced up at the house, removed his trilby, and walked up the driveway. Hayden met him at the door.

'Friends of yours?' said Lou Brannigan.

Hayden relaxed. There's nothing like not having your penis doused with boiling Assam to give you a fresh take on the sheer pleasure of being alive. The quips that had been stifled while the Twins were visiting could now be given free rein. 'Friends of yours?' didn't suggest an immediate riposte, but he was ready for repartee. And a nice cup of – aha!

'They dropped by for a nice cup of tea,' he quipped. Not bad for an opening gambit.

'I see,' said Brannigan. 'Pot empty, is it?'

'*Au contraire,*' said Hayden. 'It's a four-minute brew. They couldn't wait. Off to murder someone. Or rob a bank. They weren't specific. Or' – he was feeling positively skittish now that the pressure on his manhood was off – 'they might have had designs on some local feline.' He almost said pussy, but he was better than that. It's one of the reasons he struggled in his work. Bit too cerebral for the common taste. Unlike Foetus O'Flaherty who, at this precise moment, was wowing a live audience on lunchtime TV[6] with his roguish Irish charm and just-the-right-side-of-naughty quipettes.

'You'll be referring to the fine lady's pussycat, maybe?' said Lou Brannigan.

'You could read it that way, I suppose,' said Hayden.

'Well fair dinkum o'dooleys,' said Brannigan. 'You brought the subject up before I did. Because that's why I'm here. Your Uncle Eddie's dog, d'ye see?'

'What dog?' said Hayden.

---

[6] The BBC's *Seaside Roadshow*, live from sunny Cleethorpes.

'Don't play the wide-eyed innocent with me, Mister,' said Brannigan, wandering around the kitchen like a cop. 'His bow-wow. Rusty. Will you lookit here. A doggy bowl. A shelf-full of what's known in the grocery business as dog food. D'ye think the bould Eddie gets down on the floor there and ates the stuff himself?'

'Eddie is dead.'

'My apologies,' said Brannigan. 'Mea culpa. Sorry for your loss. I forgot. Murdered, wasn't it? Or have you copped on to yourself yet?'

'If you mean do I think he fell to his death through natural causes then no, I haven't.'

Brannigan, suddenly animated, jerked Hayden back onto Eddie's chair.

'You're getting to be a bit of an irritant round these here parts, honey boy,' he hissed. 'So here's the deal. We have reason to believe Eddie's old pal Rusty has gone native. You rein that mongrel in pronto, or next time' – he picked the pot of tea up and poured it over Hayden's crotch – 'we'll maybe settle for the ten-second brew.' Pot half-drained, he clattered it down on the hob and adjusted his trilby. 'I'll see myself out.'

14

Hayden's trousers sat drying on Eddie's chair. He was extremely upset – and no wonder. The criminal fraternity and the custodians of law and order were wreaking havoc with Eddie's teapot. Plus, Steve the barman had mentioned spare underpants; no mention of spare trousers. As if that wasn't enough, Lou Brannigan seemed to think Eddie's non-existent dog was a cat killer. To be fair, the stuff about the dog food was incontrovertible. Having said that, Brannigan seemed to know a lot more about Eddie's supposed mutt than Hayden did. If Brannigan wasn't above getting involved in the sex trade, perhaps he'd planted the dog food as evidence. The whole thing was ridiculous but maybe, just maybe, this was Brannigan's version of *Verschiebung*. He was trying to divert attention from his failure to spot a heinous crime in his jurisdiction, not to mention the fact that he was a pimp. Double *Verschiebung*.

'You planted the dog food,' barked Hayden in an authoritative voice, slightly undercut by the fact that he wasn't wearing trousers. 'You also planted the bowl. Your one oversight, my dear inspector? You forgot to plant the dog.'

Hayden's trousers continued drying slowly on the chair. Outside, the sun moved slowly across the sky. At precisely 16.32, Eddie's statue resembled, for exactly twelve seconds, a modernist Sheela-na-gig. One of Eddie's little *jeux d'esprit*, but as Hayden was inside at the time it's hardly relevant to the plot.

The sun moved ever on. Eddie's statue settled down. Hayden didn't. His life had become incredibly complicated and potentially pretty frightening in the space of a few hours. For instance, what if the Pope clan was lying in wait, following his every move? Beautiful evening for a walk, though, so Clontarf had its compensations. He managed to sublimate his terror as he took a right turn out of Eddie's, down towards Castle Avenue. Professor Emeritus Stern cycled past him in the opposite direction, presumably on his way back from a lecture, but Hayden didn't notice. I did, but this is Hayden's story. He was too busy trying to unravel the complexities of his life. Particularly the bit coming up. Here is his thinking in distilled form: if the Popes killed Eddie, and Hayden shops them to the guards, he's in big trouble. If Brannigan killed Eddie, and he shops Brannigan to himself, he's still in big trouble.

Hayden was just passing the ancient graveyard in the grounds of Clontarf Castle, mulling this over, when his mobile rang. Caller unknown. He walked absently into the graveyard, pressed answer, and put the phone to his ear.

'Yes?'

'Oh, hi. I went to the gig in Camden. Where were you?'

Shit. AA Trace.

Shit Two. He'd missed a gig in Camden.

She seemed to know more about him than he did.

'I was elsewhere,' said Hayden, curtly.

'But you were booked,' said Trace, a hint of petulance in her voice. 'Oh, and they're showing repeats of your TV thing. You know. Whatsit.'

'Sorry,' said Hayden, 'but what's whatsit?'

'*You* know,' said Trace. 'It's on E114.' She put on her best comedy voice; Geordie for some reason. '"E114. It's Toxic!"' Back to Trace-speak. 'The paedophile priest thingy.'

Hayden squirmed. *Father Brown's Boys.* Hayden had played Father 'Gormless' O'Gorman. The basic premise: two priests on an island running a home for young boys. Luckily for him, his minor character was moved to a safe parish after the pilot episode. Still. It was part of a past he was desperate to forget and, until that moment, had.

'I forbid you to watch it,' he said.

'But you're *cute*,' said Trace. 'You know something? I bet those boys were secretly pleased. Not that what you did was right, but still.' She sighed and changed the subject. 'I don't like you over there on your own, Hayden. And by the way, how's the Eight Point Plan coming along?'

Hayden thought two things. Firstly, he didn't do what he did. Father O'Gorman did. Secondly, he thought, eight? Surely it was the Twelve Point Plan. He was about to question her grasp of simple arithmetic when he passed a freshly dug grave and a wintery chill descended. Not on Clontarf. On him. Because graves reminded him of death and death reminded him of his recent visitors. It was a small step from a pot of tea on the crotch to a bullet in the cranium.

'Got to go,' he said, and ended the call. He peered into the hole and examined the mound of displaced earth. Who was it for? He didn't know, and he didn't want to know. Death, particularly at the moment, was not his sort of thing.

Anger, however, was. Had post-Catholic Ireland lost its moral compass? Prostitution, or so it seemed to Hayden, was no longer a hellfire and damnation issue. Governments around the world were adopting the so-called Babylonian model, which sought to address the problem by encouraging it, and Ireland was leading by example. The criminal underworld and law enforcement, thanks to Lou Brannigan, were one side of the same coin. As if that wasn't bad enough – although Hayden was oblivious to this bit – Professor Emeritus Stern had taken to cycling on the pavement.

Hayden felt a welling up of righteous ire. A fresh sense of purpose. A reinvigorated mission. It was a sultry evening and he was wearing sandals, but he stood taller in his metaphorical boots. This was an epiphanic moment. He, Hayden McGlynn, was on a quest: to forge a new, post-post-Catholic Ireland with an ethical core. The thought both buoyed and terrified him. He turned back up Eddie's driveway to see yet another man at the door. Hayden was rattled by thoughts of death, but the man looked harmless enough.

'Yes? Can I help you?'

The man yelped with alarm and turned to face Hayden. He had a round face and watery, colourless eyes. He stood meekly to attention, clutching an imaginary cap at chest level. Both hands.

'Ah hello,' he said. 'My name is Pascal O'Dea. I wonder if I could come in for a little-bitty minute?'

Hayden felt quite kindly towards the man. No hint of hidden menace. Not the sort to empty a teapot over your crotch. Having said that, Hayden had no intention of inviting him in. What if he was a brush salesman, the inside of his gaberdine lined with samples? If he wasn't a brush salesman, why was he wearing a coat?

'Thanks, but not interested,' said Hayden, motioning him out of the way with his front door key.

Pascal O'Dea moved meekly aside and rearranged the gaberdine belt under his armpits. Quite a refreshing response after his recent experience, so Hayden felt another twinge of guilt. He'd possibly been a bit brusque, but Pascal O'Dea didn't seem to notice.

'It's just that, well,' he said, 'I have a bit of a confession to make.'

'Try a priest,' quipped Hayden. 'I'm sure they could use the business.'

Pascal O'Dea covered his face with a pale hand and sniggered. He removed the hand and replaced it with a slightly deranged glint in his eye.

'I killed your Uncle Eddie with malice aforethought.'

Hayden lowered the key. 'Excuse me?' he said. 'Could you repeat that?'

'I killed your uncle,' said Pascal, 'with –'

'I thought that's what you said.'

Hayden was flummoxed. How did this man know Eddie had been murdered? And how could he possibly have done it? He positively oozed meek. And besides, the name: Pascal? Pascals are not killers. Pascals are... *meek*. The meek don't murder. The meek are... the meek are blessèd. Or perhaps he was hiding behind the name and the description? Hayden gave him a closer look. No. 'Meek' about summed him up. Early fifties. Lived with his mother. The centre parting – dead giveaway.

Obviously a fantasist, but still. Hayden feigned shock. 'I knew there was *something* fishy about his death,' he said. 'Poison, was it?'

'Ah no,' said Pascal, twiddling his imaginary cap nervously, 'I sawed through his ladder to the cellar. Left it, you might say, *almost* sawn through. Almost but not quite, so I was well out of the way when I achieved my goal, so to speak.' He tittered at the audacity of it. 'Oh, I did for him all right.' He tittered again. Slightly higher pitch this time. The watery eyes filled with – what? Hayden tried to put a name to it. Lunacy? 'Yes indeedy. That gent's a gonner and no mistake. He won't get up from *that* in a hurry. Thanks to yours truly.'

'But – *why?*'

Pascal moved closer and hitched up his gaberdine belt. 'I used to drop by in the mornings and switch the air on his bicycle. You need to keep it fresh, you see, otherwise it rots the inner tube. But hah! The thanks I got. He accused me of meddling. As if I would! He accused me of gawping in at his windows, if you please. As if I'm the type.' Hayden studied him closely. He *was* the type. 'He barred me from the vicinity of his hereditament. The inner tubes, says he, can look after themselves. Well I wasn't having it! No sirree bob. *Because they can't! The inner tubes cannot look after themselves!* So the point is, *Mr. Hayden McGlynn*, your uncle was a bit of a head-in-the-clouds class of a gent. He was forever *leaving the key in the fizzin door!*' Pascal tittered again, possibly hysterically this time. 'Well, that was his big mistake. I awaited my chance, so I did, and pretty soon he was off out, canvas under one arm, paint brush under the other, whistling away goodo. Brief interlude till the whistling died off and in I went, cool as you like, sawed the steps till they wouldn't bear his weight, the big eejit, back out, home again home again jiggidy jig, made the mammy her tea,' – he hugged himself with delight – '*and awaited developments with interest*.'

Hayden couldn't believe it. Pascal O'Dea was clearly deranged but, equally clearly, dangerous. It seemed impossible that such a timid little man could do such a thing, but how else would he know about the sawn-through steps? His motive was bizarre but, given his mental state, plausible. He'd got the details right. Case presumably solved, which came as a huge relief to Hayden. He didn't have to pursue Lou Brannigan *or* the Popes. In fact, it had all been much too easy. That was the trouble with crime fiction. You had to make it interesting. Plot twists and so on. Sometimes in real life, and Hayden was thinking of this case in particular, there was no plot. Twisted or otherwise.

It was an easy matter getting Pascal O'Dea to come inside and sign a full, detailed confession. He exulted in his crime. More than happy to help. In many ways the perfect crime for Lou Brannigan. He wouldn't even have to remove his boots from the desk. Hayden thanked Pascal for his commendable honesty, said the authorities would no doubt be in touch in due course, and saw him to the door.

'Sorry again about the tea,' he said. 'I've just run out.' This was a lie, but the trauma of the teapot incident was still fresh in his mind. He wasn't about to trust a third party, any third party, near the teapot. No matter how seemingly meek.

Pascal walked towards the side of the house. Hayden pointed at the gate.

'Exit's that way,' he said.

Pascal turned and smiled unctuously. 'A little job to do first,' he simpered, delving into his gaberdine's hand-stitched-by-the-mammy inside pocket. 'But don't worry. I've brought my own pump.'

15

Hayden had set out the next day with the confession transcribed and signed on Eddie's best vellum. He'd intended to drop into the Garda station, hand the confession to Lou Brannigan and become forever free of his sense of duty towards his Uncle Eddie. But Brannigan was off for the rest of the week and Hayden didn't want to leave the signed confession at the front desk. What if they lost it? Besides, he wanted to see the look on Brannigan's face when he was proved wrong. Eddie *had* been murdered.

The confession could wait. He patted his breast pocket affectionately and turned his attention back to his book. If he gave it his full attention now that the Eddie case was solved, he'd have something readable in no time. So that, you might be forgiven for thinking, was Hayden sorted. Did it all run smoothly as planned? Not quite. He did the usual thing writers do with a blank page. Ignored it. A good deal of time was spent staring out the window at Eddie's fruit trees and the statue. The latter he found mesmeric. As the sun moved slowly across the sky, it seemed to change shape in extraordinarily subtle ways. At 11.27, for example, it bore an uncanny resemblance to iconic suffragette Hanna Sheehy-Skeffington. At 13.01, 14.36 and 15.12 respectively, it appeared to have metamorphosed into Gráinne O'Malley, Maureen Potter and Eileen Gray.

The hours between were spent engrossed in yet another novel he hadn't written himself. He sat there wordless for what seemed like weeks – twelve minutes in real time – and then, undaunted, refreshed himself with a quick blurb from the back of one of Bram's books. Seconds later – three hours in real time – he'd unmasked the culprit. A Norwegian novel called *Perp*, about a man who becomes obsessed with the fact that everyone is stealing his woodpile. Not true. He's delusional, but he decides to nick it back anyway. The cops are closing in but, just as he's about to be unmasked as the biggest serial wood thief since the log stove was introduced into Scandinavia by the Vikings, the woodpile collapses and kills him. It's positively Lutheran in its take on private morality and public rectitude.

The film version starred none other than our very own Wolfe Swift, lauded as the finest screen actor of this or, arguably, any other age. Method actor of genius, he's known for total immersion, inhabiting every part. For *Perp* he learned Norwegian and manufactured a dispute with the Nordic Federation of Lumberjacks which led to an unfortunate incident with a buzz saw. The film shoot was delayed for three years while Swift served his time. In character.

But the book. Hayden put it down and returned to his own blank page.

Nothing.

On the other hand, he'd solved Eddie's murder, so a pretty good week all round.

I know I've been guilty of taking my authorial eye off the story at times. With Eddie's murderer unmasked, however, and Hayden wrestling with his own story over the next few days, I had to answer the big question: which story should I follow? The tension of the one I'd embarked on had started to sag like overused underpant elastic. I was left with a choice:

• Bin it.
• Take a short break and indulge my thirst for knowledge.

I chose the latter. A short break was exactly what was needed, and I had the very idea as to how I'd spend the time. I'd seen Professor Stern cycling off in the mornings, presumably to his office at City of Dublin University. I checked their website to see if the learned Professor was holding a summer course in comedic arts. Theory? Practice? Who cared. It's a vast subject, and Professor Stern embraces its vastness in several seminal works. In *Beyond Tragedy*, for instance, he explores areas you almost wish he didn't. Nothing on the website, but maybe they thought they'd be inundated. Word of mouth alone would more than fill a course run by this intellectual colossus. With Hayden seemingly settled in for the day, I took this as the perfect opportunity to borrow Eddie's bike and cycle off in search of cultural stimuli. With any luck, I'd return the bike before Hayden noticed it was gone.

The bicycle was sturdy, though slightly lumbering and in need of a good dose of oil. On the plus side, the tyres were firm and full of fresh air thanks to Pascal. I benefited from a tail wind along Kincora Road and past Herr Schrödinger's, struggled up Castle Avenue, and approached Killester with some relief. Collins Avenue is gradient-free, and there, at the Ballymun Road end, my cycle ended. City of Dublin University. Bright, modern, buzzy.

I didn't have a padlock for the bike, so I wheeled it into reception. They assumed, apparently, that I was a visiting academic, so this was deemed an endearing eccentricity. The assumption was inaccurate but understandable. Adjectives used to describe me include 'cultured', 'raffish', and, on one memorable occasion involving the chairwoman of a Surrendered Wives conference in Dunfanaghy and a misunderstanding over seating arrangements, 'predatory'. The blue-haired young receptionist couldn't have been more helpful. Until, that is, she discovered the reason for my visit. The lowering of status from visiting intellectual with bicycle clips to mere would-be mature student, also with bicycle clips, was transparent.

Was Professor Emeritus Stern, I asked, holding any short summer courses? A self-contained weekend for comedy Level Fives, I suggested, would be ideal. The receptionist, Áine Ní Cheannáin if her name badge was to be believed, peered at me over a pair of imaginary half-frame glasses.

'I'm afraid we don't have a Professor Stern in situ at this particular facility. Emeritus or otherwise. And bicycles are not permitted on the premises.'

Pithy, I'll give her that. She was about to return to her work, but I was ahead of her.

'Perhaps you could double-check,' I said. 'Professor Emeritus Larry Stern. Department of Comedic Arts. City of Dublin University. It says so on his website.'

'I'm sure it does,' said Ms Ní Cheannáin. 'I think you'll find, however, that this is University of Dublin City, not City of Dublin ditto. UDC[7], if you will, not CDU. I haven't heard of a CDU myself.' She removed her glasses, still imaginary, and gave me the full Ní Cheannáin go thither stare. 'Nor am I au fait with their current policy vis-à-vis bicycles in the foyer. If, indeed, they exist in the first place. And finally, regarding the Department of Comedic Arts,' she may have trembled with emotion at this point, 'we don't facilitate, nor have we ever to my almost certain knowledge facilitated, any such faculty.'

My brain was in turmoil. I'd made a basic error. I'd superimposed one university on the other. CDU on UDC. So where was CDU? I didn't feel I could ask Ms Ní Cheannáin to check online. We didn't have that sort of relationship.

I was perplexed as I cycled back to Clontarf and replaced the bicycle against Eddie's wall. I'd seemingly mislaid City of Dublin University, yet Professor Emeritus Stern cycled off *somewhere* every morning, so somewhere is where it must be. I'd also, as I soon discovered, mislaid Hayden. He was not, as I'd hoped, strapped to his desk, busily pumping out some Celtic screwball noir. So where was he? As the author, I knew that locating him was my top priority. I shouldn't have left him alone. He'd wandered away from his desk and could be anywhere. The Nautical Buoy? Dollymount? Elsewhere?

---

[7] I've changed the name to protect the university's reputation for academic excellence. Same address, though.

I was eliminating the possibles one by one and had just reached the end of Eddie's driveway when I spotted Hayden's three aunts weeding the petunias.

'Good morning, ladies,' I said.

'It's afternoon. You artists!'

'I'll bet he doesn't know what day of the week it is eider.'

'What millennium is it, Een?'

They giggled happily, like the gurgle of water over stones on a sun-kissed mountain stream or similar. I was about to ask if they knew anything about Hayden's whereabouts when they were off again.

'We do follow your career wit interest, Een.'

'Oh, you've done very well for yourself. What was that playlet on the BBC Home Service?'

'*Prune Surprise.*'

'Very Shavian, Een.'

'We *hooted.*'

'Speaking of scribblers, Een, we seen Hayding is at it now.'

'The very man I was looking for,' I said. 'Do you lovely ladies have any idea where he is?'

'Lovely ladies indeed, Een. Duly noted.'

'You haven't lost it.'

'But to return to the subject, to wit Hayding, last we heard he was off down to Dollyer for a swimbulation.'

'In the sea, the snotgreen sea, the scrotumtightening sea.'

'That's only a quote, by the way, but it puts *us* off.'

'Not that we have scrotums, mind you. It's the principle of the ting.'

'Clitoris-shrivelling more like.'

'Florrie! Spare the poor boy's blushes.'

'Dottie. And he's got to learn sometime.'

'Anyway, that's where Hayding's gone, Een.'

'In search of his autorial voice.'

'Actually.'

'*His* words.'

82

They giggled in unison at the pomposity of it all.

'Well, it's been lovely catching up, Een, but these hollyhocks aren't going to weed themselves.'

Petunias, as I said, but let it pass, let it pass.

'We'll tell Hayding we seen you. Bye now.'

And they returned to their work with nimble, arthritic fingers, and continued their three-way monologue.

'I don't know about you, Dottie, but I tought he *was* Hayding.'

'Dodie. You mean he isn't?'

'Must be the dementia. And by the way, isn't it "scrota"?'

'Oh now. Hark at you wit your Latin. You've never been the same since you got back from Argentina. It's all Gabriel García Márquez this, Gabriel García Márquez that.'

'Maria Vargas Llosa, if you don't mind. But what a truly magnificent –'

'Point of information. I tink you're referring to *Mario.*'

'You could be right at that. There *was* someting fishy about her lower bits.'

I zoned out. I'd just spotted Hayden approaching with a wet towel draped over his shoulder and a positive spring in his step, whistling merrily and twirling his togs.

I resolved not to lose him again.

16

Hayden thought of going down to the Garda station as soon as Brannigan got back the following Monday, but as things turned out it's just as well he didn't.

After a long lie-in brought on by a feeling of wellbeing, he opted instead to listen to an Eddie reel-to-reeler with a late breakfast of beans on toast, a childhood favourite, and one of the few things Eddie had known how to cook. He'd then pop back to the station, whack the confession down in front of Lou Brannigan, and see what he made of *that.*

The tape. Eddie's voice in conversation with a world-weary male circa 1956 fills the room. On the recording, Eddie then plays an earlier tape of himself listening to a still-earlier tape. Riveting stuff: Eddie and friend listening to Eddie listening to himself. Sounds complicated, but it's a pre-post-postmodern joy, and decades ahead of its time. Eddie chuckles with pleasure.

'Bit solipsistic, mebbe? What do you reckon, Sam?'

Then Sam's voice, a totally different Sam from the earlier, world-weary version: 'This – this is *brilliant!!!* Mind if I use it?'

'Fire away, Sam. No use it just sitting there. Plenty more ideas where that came from. Glad you like it. Be my guest.' Eddie's artless delight in the compliment, not to mention his generosity of spirit, is both admirable and strangely touching.

At which point Sam pleads a prior engagement and rushes off. Tape ends.

Hayden shook his head in wonder. Uncle Eddie. 'Sam'. Was there no end to Eddie's talent? To his influence? It stirred up strange feelings of familial pride and – difficult to know what the other feeling was, but it felt in some strange way ungenerous, and it made him doubly keen to re-engage with his own work. He set about sorting some more of the clutter on Eddie's desk, including several notebooks detailing future projects. Inside one, a loose photo of a reddish brown, open-faced dog. Big eyes. Trusting look. Slightly lop-sided face, possibly due to the left ear being set at a jaunty angle. A classic thoroughbred mongrel. On the facing page, the following:

Lines Written in Celebration of an Everlasting Bond
Eddie McGlynn & Rusty

Here lies a ribald, crusty knave

Who never stooped to beg.

His dog is known to use the grave

To cock an idle leg.

Both knave and beast were man and mate

When master walked above.

So does the one now urinate

To show the other love?

In spite of himself, Hayden was deeply moved. The world had moved on from rhyming verse and its illegitimate offspring, doggerel, but there was something refreshingly direct about this simple verse. Something indefinable. Perhaps it was the picture of a trusting little pooch, with his big eyes and that look which Hayden recognised immediately – as if it spoke to some deep, missing need in Hayden himself – of unconditional love.

He was about to read it again, in search of possible clues, when he heard a distinct scratching sound coming from outside. He followed it to the front door.

'Hello?'

He felt slightly foolish. It was hardly a human scratch. Closer to ground level. And why would a human bother scratching when there was a perfectly serviceable bell and knocker?

You're probably ahead of our hero. Verse about a dog? Scratching? Hayden opened the door. Two things sat on the porch:

- A large cardboard box with a note attached that said '*We called but you were out*', which he wasn't, or he'd have fallen over it on the way back in.
- Rusty.

At least Hayden assumed it was Rusty. A sad-eyed russet mutt, with one floppy ear and one ear standing to attention, sat whining softly beside the cardboard box. Hayden motioned him in, but he stayed where he was, his doleful eyes trained on the box. Hayden picked it up and went inside, leaving the door open. Interesting. Rusty didn't just come in: he seemed to follow the box. Hayden placed it on the desk and opened a tin of a well-known brand of dog food. By Royal Appointment to Her Majesty the Queen, apparently. If it was good enough for Her Majesty, you'd have thought...

He slopped some into the dog bowl. No movement from Rusty, who seemed fixated on the box, so he set about opening it. Inside, a smaller cardboard box. He set about opening that.

Straw.

Bubble wrap.

Urn.

Uncle Eddie had arrived home.

Hayden placed the urn on the kitchen unit and turned his attention to Rusty. Rusty sat beside the bowl, totally oblivious to its royal seal of approval, staring with still-doleful eyes straight at Eddie's ashes.

Hayden suddenly understood. Rusty, that most faithful of animals, had spent the past week searching for Eddie's grave in the traditional way. Coffin, burial, conventional graveyard. No luck. Whatever adventures he'd had, and whatever characters he'd met, he'd failed to find the object of his search. Undaunted, he'd followed his instincts, been advised by some wise old animals and bird life along the way and found himself back at Eddie's at the precise moment that Eddie, in his urn, arrived back too. Sound plausible? I hope so, because I've written a children's book on that very theme[8] – although to be honest I haven't had a great deal of success with children's publishers up to now, and, based on the first few responses back from literary agents, I'm not convinced my luck is about to change.

Rusty, meanwhile, sighed tragically, his eyes fixed inconsolably on Eddie's urn, the doggy bowl untouched. Hayden was moved by compassion and an understandable desire to get as far away as possible from his desk.

It took some time to find a dog lead, attach it to Rusty and convince him to leave his beloved master. Apparently Rusty and the Queen didn't share the same taste in dog food, so the plan was to pop down to Madden's, see what was on offer. Several lamp posts later – perfect scene for a kids' book, but dog willies and wee-wee are of no concern to us here – Hayden tied Rusty's lead to a bicycle stand near the main entrance of the supermarket and went inside. Rusty sat and awaited Hayden's return, his large, melancholy eyes attracting pats on the head and the usual 'who's-a-good-doggie' stuff as Hayden stood deep in thought in the dog food section. Decisions, decisions. He was weighing up the merits and demerits of a self-styled 'leading' brand and Madden's own make – both rich in bone-strengthening marrowbone jelly, for those interested in such matters – when the three aunts scurried past and disappeared down the next aisle.

Were they trying to avoid him? They *must* have seen him. He hurried past the special offers and cut them off as they scuttled along the toiletry aisle.

[8] *Rapscallion.*

'Ladies, ladies, ladies,' he said. 'What an unexpected pleasure.'

If they were surprised, they didn't show it.

'Why, it's our friendly neighbourhood sloot.'

'Are you a sloot? Are you, Hayding?'

'A private dick, pardon our French.'

They may have been about to launch into more prattle, but Hayden interrupted. He produced Pascal O'Dea's confession from his breast pocket and waved it playfully across their startled faces.

'*Ex*-dick, my dears. I rather fancy I may have just solved the case.'

This was a new Hayden, an effervescent Hayden, and the effect on the three aunts couldn't have been more pleasing. They rocked back on their carpet slippers in total silence, perhaps for the first time in their long, long lives. They processed the information like wizened anglerfish, and Hayden savoured the moment. They'd had their fun with him, but now? Hah. He was about to confide that he'd have to speak to the relevant authorities first before winding up proceedings, when he heard a familiar voice in the next aisle over.

'I assassinated President Kennedy, Mr. Madden.'

'Of course you did, Pascal. Of course you did. And I suppose you bumped his big brother off too?'

Pascal's falsetto titter was unlike any sound Hayden had ever heard.

'You knew!'

'That's a good boy, Pascal,' said Mr. Madden. 'Go home to your mammy now and try to stop killing people. It's not nice.'

The three aunts were giggling again.

'That makes tirty people he's killed this week, Hayding. And counting.'

'So anyway. You were saying.'

Hayden put the confession back in his pocket. 'It's... it's all a bit speculative at the moment. Early... early days.'

His body language had changed. Playful fled to be replaced by tentative, as he dredged up his first encounter with Pascal from his subconscious. Not, as his conscious mind had deduced, at the front door of Eddie's house, but before that, deep in conversation with Bram at the Nautical Buoy. '*Is anyone using the salt?*' Those simpering tones – it couldn't have been anyone else.

Hayden was back at square one, he knew it, and the aunts, sensing the change in the atmosphere, seemed to know it too.

'The mystery is not quite soluted yet we humbly submit, Hayding.'

'And sometimes, whisper it softly,' – there was something in the way they said this that gave it a certain resonance – 'a mystery is best left unsoluted.'

'But look. Quilted toilet rolls fifty centimetres off, so it's not all bad news.'

They grabbed a packet and shuffled off to the alcohol section.

'To replenish our stocks, Hayding.'

'Just in case.'

'You simply never know.'

Dottie, or it may have been Florrie – the strip lighting was on the blink – nudged him affectionately with a bony finger as they left. Hayden, deflated as only the recently smug can truly be, trudged back to the dog food.

He opted eventually for Madden's own-brand Turkey Brunch, and proceeded to fill his basket with bread, tins of tuna, a week's supply of loose-leaf Assam and a two-pack of budget toilet roll, non-quilted; but his heart wasn't in it.

He headed to the tills. The three aunts had got there before him. He was about to duck behind a display of disposable nappies until they'd gone when they spotted him again.

'There you are, Hayding. We've been coo-eeing you for yonks.'

'The lovely checkout lady wants proof of age. Isn't that gas?'

It was now Hayden's turn to rock back on his heels.

'I was merely trying to make them reconsider the cooking sherry,' said Trace. 'That stuff ruined my life.'

'What the' – Hayden cut the fuck word just in time – 'are *you* doing here?'

Trace's reproachful eyes bored through him.

'I was worried about you,' she said, 'so I came over. Thought I might be here for a while so, you know, there was this job going...'

Before Hayden could splutter an outraged response, the three aunts were off.

'Oh now. You never told us you had a young lady, Hayding.'

'Well aren't you the dark horse? And there was us tinking you were gay.'

'No harm in that, mind. We seem to remember one of *us* is gay, Hayding. It's not you is it, Florrie?'

'Not unless Orsing Welles was a lady. And I'm not sure I'm Florrie eider.'

But Hayden wasn't listening. He was glowering at Trace. Trace returned his glower with a defiant look.

'You're a lost soul, Hayden,' she said, 'and I'm your guardian angel. Like in that movie. What's it called again?'

'*Stalker.*'

The word had been festering in his mind for some time. Now it was out. It had the intended effect.

'That's not nice, Hayden,' said Trace in a very small voice. 'It's... it's *hurtful.* Oh, and by the way,' her voice now back to normal, 'I got you these.'

She produced a packet from under the counter and thrust it at him. He threw the packet with malice aforethought on the grocery belt, which sent it back to Trace.

'Underpants,' she said. 'Three-for-two.' She stopped the belt and pushed them back to Hayden. 'You'll thank me tomorrow.'

The three aunts were lost in a reverie.

'Underpants, Hayding. That is *so* romantic.'

*

Hayden's brain hurt. A jumble of thoughts and people, all vying for space. He would have discussed these with Rusty on the way back to Eddie's if he hadn't left him outside the supermarket. He noted the oversight when he was halfway back, and returned, chastened, to Madden's. The three aunts were fussing over the grieving dog.

'There you are, Hayding, and not a moment too soon.'

'Traumatised, he was.'

'A dirty great tabby squaring up to him.'

'Hissing like a ruddy adder, Hayding. And there he was stuck on his doggy lead. Mesmerised.'

'We tink he might have wet himself, Hayding.'

'Or maybe not. Can you wet yourself if you don't wear pants? Discuss.'

They were about to set off down the giggle route again. Hayden unwound the lead and feigned nonchalance.

'Thanks,' he said. 'I've had a lot on my mind recently, but here, give me your bags and I'll see you home.'

'Pass the toot, Hayding, as we say in French. You run on ahead now, like a good boy.'

'You'll be up to your slooty eyeballs in slooting.'

'Looking for fresh leads and so fort.'

They patted a still traumatised Rusty.

'No pun intended.'

Hayden examined their puckered little faces to see if they betrayed any signs of mockery. They didn't, on the surface anyway, but he was followed up Vernon Avenue by the tintin-nabulating sound of girlish laughter.

The tabby cat encounter was a potentially interesting development. On its own it may have added little, but consider the following: as Hayden and Rusty entered the home stretch, a large, well-fed ginger tom sitting on a nearby wall eyeballed Rusty lazily as he passed. Typical Clontarf cat. Proprietorial. Urbane in tooth and claw. Rusty cowered and gave it a wide berth. Simultaneously, and just as Hayden turned into Eddie's driveway, a man further along the road stopped at his garden gate and banged, discreetly, on a cat-food tin. The ginger tom yawned, slithered off the wall, stretched and followed the tin.

Different cat, same response from Rusty: aversion to conflict. Why is this interesting? Rusty, it suggested, was no cat killer.

17

F ast forward ten minutes. Hayden was trying to get Rusty to eat. Turkey Brunch, yummy yummy. Marrowbone jelly, mnnnn. As a desperate last resort, he led by example, taking a few bites himself. Mnnnn, yummy yummy, mnnnn. But his attention was elsewhere. Pascal O'Dea's confession now lay scrunched in a ball on top of the waste basket, useless. Hayden was furious. The three aunts were delighted with their 'slooting' jibes, but he'd show 'em. He wouldn't rest until Eddie's murder was slooted.

'Slooted, ladies. Finally, irrevocably, definitively. What do you have to say to *that*?' Nothing! That's what they'd have to say to that.

As soon as he'd established that Rusty wasn't interested in Madden's award-winning Turkey Brunch, he put the remains of the tin in the fridge, filled the kettle, laid out the tea tray and opened his notebook. He drew a line down the page. One side: In The Frame. Other side: Not In The Frame. In The Frame? Brannigan. The Popes. Marina. Possibly Brannigan *and* Marina. Person or persons unknown. Not In The Frame? Pascal O'Dea.

It was a start.

He wet the tea, sat back down and drummed his fingers on the desk. Hayden in pensive mode. Four minutes passed. He'd forgotten all about the tea as he tried to work out who Eddie might have upset over the years. The church. The arts establishment. Ah! His parents. But hold on; they were in Waikiki at the time of Eddie's death. End of that line of enquiry. He placed them neatly in Not In The Frame, which now read:

- Pascal.

- Mother.
- Father.

He'd split his parents up to make it look as if he was getting somewhere, which he wasn't. He found it impossible to sleep that night, no further forward with his lines of enquiry, no further forward with his book.

It was after midnight. Hayden was engrossed in the *More Sam* tape, which gave an added piquancy to the Eddie/Sam relationship. The final section involves an altercation between Eddie and leading literary critic PJ O'Malley.[9] A tetchy PJ was furious with Eddie 'for having the audacity to influence the pre-eminent playwright of the twentieth century [*sic*]. It upsets the dominant narrative,' he spluttered. 'You're undermining the reputation of the man I love.' It gets worse. 'You'll live to regret it, because let me tell you this: I have the contacts.'

The recording ends with the celebrated critic's petulant refusal of a Sweet Ambrosia top-up on the grounds that he hadn't accepted a drink in the first place, and the pitter-patter of cerebral feet as he flounced to the exit. Hayden didn't bother adding his name to the possible suspect list. PJ O'Malley had the contacts? He was probably referring to the *London Review of Books*.

Hayden was having a quiet chuckle about this when the front doorbell rang. No response from a terminally depressed Rusty, not even a twitch of his good ear, but Hayden tensed up. It was 01.27, well outside visiting hours; unless, of course, the under-cover-of-darkness factor applied, in which case it wasn't. He put the light out, crept softly to the door and listened. He expected the tuneless whistling of Lou Brannigan, or the menacing silence of the Popes. But no. All he could make out was a high-pitched chirruping sound; a bit like the Dublin Zoo bird enclosure at feeding time. The doorbell rang again.

[9] Pre-order your copy of *The Annotated Sloot* now for the full transcript.

'Coo-ee, Hayding. We know you're in there.'

He braced himself and opened up. What the hell did *they* want at this hour?

'Aren't you going to invite your old aunties in?'

'It's very dark out here. We could be abducted, Hayding.'

Hayden examined his wrist pointedly.

'One tirty, Hayding. On the dot.'

'We'll just squeeze past.'

Hayden ushered them in with the long-suffering sigh he reserved for his three beloved aunts and global catastrophes, and followed them into the living room. He assumed they'd come for a reason, but you never knew. They lit on the tape box and suddenly went quiet. Not that it stopped them talking.

'What's this? I tought you filed all Eddie's tapes away, Dottie.'

'Dodie. And that, as I recall, was your job.'

Hayden detected a distinct edge to this little exchange. They turned, possibly accusingly, towards him. Something told him to act dumb, so he did. You don't tell your aunts *anything* they don't need to know. Tapes? What tapes? Nothing to do with me, guv. They seemed relieved.

'Well anyway, Hayding, bit of an oversight, we conclude, so back on the shelf it goes.'

What was all that about? Hayden had no idea. Task completed, however, they seemed to revert to their sweetly batty little selves.

'*More Sam*, dough. Remember Samuel, ladies?'

'We do indeed.'

'Indeed we do.'

'Swanned off to Paris, Hayding.'

'Done *very* well for himself.'

'A wonderfully experimental lover as I recall. He was certingly ahead of the curve on gender identity.'

'Happy day, dough. Happy days.'

'*Happy Days* indeed, Hayding. That's what he was working on at the time.'

'Metod writing. Asked us to call him Winnie.'

Hayden raised a hand for silence. This, he felt, could go on all night. 'What can I do for you, ladies?' he asked.

They seemed relieved to change the subject.

'A very good and apposite question, Hayding. Only we seen the urn being delivered.'

'We didn't want to intrude on private grief.'

'But we're here to carry out our dear departed brudder Eddie's express wishes.'

'To recapitulate, Hayding. The Hellfire Club, deep in the heart of the Dubling Mountings. First full moon. Tree tirty-tree.'

'Beelzebub here I come, quote unquote.'

'Wasn't he gas, though?'

'A hoot,' scowled Hayden.

'Tree tirty-tree be the light of the moon.'

'The mooon, Hayding.'

'The moooooon!'

Rusty may have been about to join in, indeed it might well have contributed to the healing process for the poor dog, but Hayden had had enough.

'Stop it,' he snapped. 'You're unnerving me.'

'Well, come on then.'

'Grab the urn, stick it in this Madden's bag for life –'

'– which, by the way, we'd like back as we've been monitoring its longevity –'

'– and let's skedaddle. Tempus is fugiting fast.'

They rattled a set of car keys and cackled happily.

'The broomstick is parked on the roof.'

18

The broomstick, it turned out, was a pink Mini. 1963 reg. The three aunts drove. Possibly all three at once. It was that kind of drive. For Hayden and Rusty it was a traumatic experience: a bare-knuckle ride surrounded by over-excited ancients. This sort of thing is standard cinematic fare for devotees of Level One[10], but not so funny if you have to live through it – which Hayden and Rusty did. They also had to sit through some pretty explicit reminiscences involving long-forgotten pop stars of 1960's vintage, the three aunts, and the back seat of the Mini. I hope I never succumb to the urge to write them down, but if ever I do, I promise to observe the thirty-year rule.

Skip this bit if you have no interest in silent cinema, comic genius or early twentieth century left-wing politics. Before you do, however, know this: you ought to be ashamed of yourself. I'm almost tempted to tell you who – if anyone – killed Eddie, because quite frankly The Inquisitive Bullet narrative deserves a better class of reader. But that would mean spoiling the story for the rest of us, and I'm not prepared to do that.

In a fit of skittishness, the three aunts stopped the car on the tram tracks at Amiens Street station. Smack in the centre of Dublin.

'Oh no, Hayding. We're stuck.'

'Get out and push or we'll all be deaded.'

---

[10] Prof. Larry Stern, *Laughter and Wealth: The Lowest Common Denominator Theory of Comedy.*

'You alone can save us, we being tree wizened little ladies of a certing age and you being a big hairy man.'

'Save us.'

'For pity's sake *save u-u-u-ussss*.'

Hayden stared out the window onto the deserted street, then exchanged long-suffering glances with Rusty, who may have commiserated. He might equally have been nursing his own secret sorrow.

'The car isn't stuck,' said Hayden. 'The first tram is not for another four hours. The driver sets off from about twenty feet away and might be reasonably expected to see us in time. Need I go on?'

The venerable Mini roared into life and bounced happily off.

'Tanks, Hayding.'

'Hayding saves the day.'

'Our hero.'

I mention this because it replicates, in a quintessentially modern way, the story arc of Finlay Jameson's 1917 masterpiece, *Tram*, in which our intrepid and permanently furious hero chains himself to the tracks only to find that the tram drivers have called a three-day strike for better pay and conditions. The film in question was denied an American release – no drama – but lauded as political cinema of the highest order and compulsory viewing in the nascent USSR, leading to Finlay's so-called red phase, and the freedom of the city of Minsk. I've seen the film, all three days of it, and despite being a lifelong leftie myself, I have to admit political discourse doesn't always produce the best art. Particularly in silent cinema.

19

The foothills of the Dublin mountains. Ah, the mem'ries, the mem'ries. I'm reminded of the time... But that will have to wait for the autobiography. This, after all, is not about me.

The pink Mini bounced to a halt. Lights out. The moon shone like – I'm tempted to say like a pre-energy-saving hundred-watt light bulb. Bit clunky, but you get the drift. With a vintage hundred-watter you could read a 19th century Presbyterian bible *sans* glasses. Play a cricket match at midnight and keep the fast bowlers on. Make out every detail of the Hellfire Club, that legendary ruin on top of Mount Pelier Hill, from the front window of the three aunts' ancient car; which is exactly what Hayden did.

'Hmn,' he said. 'Bats.'

The three aunts stared at the dark creatures flitting around the craggy ruins.

'Or *are* they?'

'This we don't know, Hayding.'

'Yet.'

They turned and peered at him, in frightening unison.

'Could be the girls out for a nocturnal fly-about.'

'Around the moon, Hayding.'

'The moooon!'

'Stop it,' said Hayden. 'You're not witches. Let's get this over with.'

'You're right, Hayding. We're tree dotty oul wans wit dementia.'

And they were off again. Giggle giggle giggle, possibly cackle, and they kept it up as Hayden trudged through the bracken and pine tree stumps, up the moonlit hill towards the luminous and looming ruin. He glowered at them for a while, but soon the levels of concentration needed to negotiate the uneven ground took over. The aunts, on the other hand, seemed to skip lightly on their way, and when Hayden almost disappeared down a concealed bog hole, they hooted.

'Your little face, Hayding.'

'God, if you could do that in a fillum!'

'You'd be mega.'

'It's the way you keep it serious, Hayding. Priceless. Who's that fella we're tinking of?'

'Finlay Jamesing.'

'The very same. I mean look at you, Hayding.'

'You're wasted on the talkies.'

Here's the extraordinary thing: they were absolutely right! Professor Stern has described just such a scene in his ground-breaking study, *The Unintentionality of Comic Genius*. I wound it back in my head. Hayden struggling through stumps and bracken on his relentless forward march. Dour. Morose. Focussed. Then, out of nowhere, GLUP! Chest high in damp, millennia-old peat. No change in his facial expression if we exclude an added layer of startled humiliation. The hope, expectation and final indignity of all human life encapsulated in seventeen seconds. File under *Comedy: Level Five*. A remarkably similar scene features in Finlay Jameson's masterpiece, *The Suicide*, in which our furious anti-hero decides to end it all but is thwarted at every turn by near death experiences.

They reached the summit in ebullient mood. The aunts, that is. As if they'd been spirited down to Earth for this very moment. The ashes in their polished urn. The brooding, satanic ruin. The melancholy soughing of a light, gusting breeze. The moooooon. Hayden trudged up behind them, removing dried bracken and small lumps of peat from his bog-wet clothes. His dour and morose expression had now set into a permanent scowl.

'We know, Hayding. We know. A sad moment in many ways.'

'Yet curiously uplifting withal.'

'Because maybe Eddie would want us rather to rejoice, rejoice, rejoice as we return his ashes to the unhallowed ground from whence they heretofore sprang.'

'We're making this up as we go along, Hayding. No supplied script.'

'But here. We tink you should do the honours, you being the next generation of huming life and so on and so fort, et ceteri et cetera.'

'Not quite yet dough, Hayding.'

'Tree tirty-tree. He was very particular about that.'

Hayden felt suddenly sombre. As the sole male McGlynn currently resident in Ireland, he was technically head of the family. If, that is, we accept the patriarchal power structures which have existed in Ireland since the evolution of the penis. Hayden removed the urn from the Madden's bag for life. As his hand clasped the lid, he heard it. A terrifying primal roar, resounding through the dark, foreboding walls of the ancient ruin.

The three aunts' antennae went up.

'Jaykers. What was that?'

'It brought our maternal side up to the surface, Hayding.'

They looked momentarily startled.

'Not that we've had any children, Hayding. As such.'

Suddenly, close by, an angry human bark. Guttural with pent-up rage.

'What's that you said, Hayding?'

'*Just grab the fucken spade.*'

'Oh, very good, Hayding.'

'Perfectamundo *I'd* say. You've got the gift.'

Hayden lowered his voice to a terrified whisper. 'That wasn't me. Now can you please keep your voices down?'

But they didn't hear him. They'd suddenly shot off, straight in the direction of the sounds. Into the valley of the shadow of death rode the three aunts. At least it seemed that way to

Hayden. Righteous indignation lent them wings. Or it might, for all he knew, have been simple curiosity. He groaned, wiped a buzzard dropping from his lapel and followed, at what he hoped was a safe distance, in their wake.

20

As Hayden stepped from the shadows of the ruin into the full glow of the moonlight, he saw his aunts approach a dip in the ground. Hayden tiptoed forward, his path full of dry twigs. He knelt with exaggerated delicacy beside them and peered over the edge. Below in the dell, a dozen or so shadowy figures stood in a circle as if performing some sort of ritual.

'Gwan ya hoor ya! Dig the fucken grave!'

The three aunts were mesmerised into hushed stage whispers.

'Isn't that gas, Hayding? It's like one of those gangster fillums. Remember those?'

'Humperty Go-cart we used to call him.'

'Weenshy little scrut of a ting.'

'But what a lover!'

'No he wasn't, Dottie. You're tinking of Marlene Dietrich.'

'Dementia, Hayding. You've got to make allowances.'

'Will you please be quiet,' hissed Hayden.

'Shush, ladies. He wants to hear the scene unfolding.'

'Sorry, Hayding. I suppose you'll be putting it in your great Irish novel.'

'No,' he hissed. 'I'd just prefer it if we didn't get killed.'

'They're killing *him*, Hayding. Not us. Where's your compashing?'

'They're about to send him to an early grave, Hayding. And for why?'

'Yor bringin the whole family into disre-fucken-puhe, Frankie. Yor nor a fucken woman. I mean whar abouh childberth? Periods? Menstru-fucken-ation?'

Hayden leaned forward. He knew those voices. JP. Benny. The Pope Twins – about to kill Frankie! But surely Frankie was the criminal mastermind? The brains behind the outfit? It didn't make any sense. And what about the woman thing? That didn't make any sense either.

'You dissed the famly name when you went legih, Frankie.' Ah. Hayden understood that one. And there was more. 'Yor supposed to be launderin the fucken spondulix, noh poncin abouh wih yor bewkes an yor elocution less –'

'Give me a break, lads. I never laundered the money and okay, so I ponce about with books, but I don't take elocution lessons. I listen to Radio 4. It's not my fault if it rubs off.'

'Don't fucken interrupt. Where was I?'

The other brothers grabbed the chance to join in.

'Yor bewkes, JP.'

'Yor elocution lessons.'

'Spor on. Okay, Frankie. Fine. Fair enough. Your call. Buh wantin to be a fucken bird in – in thah fucken paintin.' Hayden was rooted to the spot. Painting? Back to JP. 'Words fucken fail me, Frankie. They fail all of us, righ? We're – we're dumbstruck, Frankie.'

Frankie placed a foot on the graveside verge and rested his elbow on his knee. Hayden was desperate to hear about the painting, but he couldn't help admiring the way Frankie was handling all this in the face of his own mortality. No teapot, but in many ways, being murdered on a lonely mountainside at dead of night and forced to dig your own grave beforehand was worse.

'You'll be havin yor bollix cuh off next, am I righ?' JP was in full impassioned flow, spurred on by his raucous siblings. 'Jus remembah, Frankie, every mickey is sacred.'

'Sperm, JP. Every *sperm* is sacred.'

'Eg-fucken-zackly.'

'Look,' Frankie said. 'The painting. I can explain it. I just did it because Eddie asked me, okay? He wanted to subvert notions of male and female in the context of –'

'In the context of yor tool,' growled JP. 'Thass a slippery slope, Frankie. The thin end of a dangerous fucken wedge. You crossed the line with the lady paintin stuff. Next thing you'll have yor testicles trussed up in swaddlin clothes til the operation an before you know ih, bang goes yor truncheon an yor a fucken moh.'[11]

The Pope clan muttered its collective approval, but Frankie was unrepentant.

'So?'

'Don't inta-fucken-rupt! It's a subject we Popes feel very strongly abouh – because here's why. Yor ah an impressionable age, Frankie.'

'I'm thirty-five, JP.'

'Exackly. Few years time you'll change yor mind. No goin back. You'll be on drugs yor whole fucken life. Sure these pharmaceutical boys have this whole thing sewn up. An you know our thinkin on drugs, Frankie.'

He clapped his fists on his stumpy thighs and drew a deep, meaningful breath.

'Drugs is for other people,' said Benny.

JP turned on him.

'Thah,' he snarled, 'was my fucken line. The piece de fucken resistance. I was pausin, ya poxy fucken afterberth ya, for dramahic fucken effect.' He slapped the side of his head in frustration and spat into the open grave. 'Clemmie. Take the fucken spade. Finish the fucken hole off. We haven't gor all fucken nigh.'

The brothers settled down. This was high drama. Clemmie winced and stepped forward. Frankie bowed theatrically and handed him the spade. Hayden studied Frankie closely. *Portrait of a Lady*. She, the lady in the painting, was none other than Frankie 'Francis' Pope. The intelligent, feminine face. The

---

[11] A 'mot', for those reading this in standard English, is a woman.

broad-for-a-woman but definably male shoulders. The imposing woman at Eddie's funeral; that had been Frankie too.

The sheer guts for a man of his background to do such a thing. Hayden was about to take his metaphorical hat off to Frankie when – the three aunts were off.

'Will you lookit who it is, girls. It's little Francis Pope. Hasn't he got very tall dough?'

'And still the outdoor sporty type, we deduce.'

'Hence, we further deduce, the extreme gardening.'

'I'll tell you one ting, Francis. You'll never get spudatoes to grow *there*.'

A fit of nonagenarian giggles as they clambered over the dip. The Popes, probably for the first time in their violent, law-disdaining lives, were rooted to the spot. As if they'd just been surprised by the Krays and discovered they were triplets.

'Who the fuck are youse?'

The three aunts tutted in unison.

'Language, Benedict.'

'It is little Benedict, isn't it?'

'There are ladies present, if we may make so bold.'

'And besides, what would your mammy tink?'

'She'd be turning in her grave if she was dead.'

'Lucky for her dough she only has gout, or she'd be here wit us tonight.'

'She has gouh?' said Benny. 'Wha the fuck is gouh?'

'Shuh fucken up, Benny,' said JP. He turned to the three aunts. 'You know the ma?'

'Indeed yes. A very old friend of ours, Big Mags. Isn't she, ladies?'

'It all harks back to our waitressing days in Bewley's Cafetooria. The Westmoreland Street branch.'

'Your mammy used to come in for afternoon tea.'

'She was very partial, I recall, to Bewley's own-make pistachio meringues.'

'Oh yes, she was a right lady, wasn't she girls? Very particular.'

'Gentility itself *I'd* say.'

'Wha? *Ma?*'

'Oh indeed. And her tips were legendary. I still have a florin she gave me in the late fifties.'

'We should have it stuffed and mounted, Dodie.'

'Florrie, Dottie.'

Dottie smiled apologetically at the Popes.

'Dementia. We've had it for as long as we can remember.'

'About twelve seconds.'

'Jesus,' said JP. 'Leh's get this ovah. On you fucken go, Clem.'

The aunts stopped giggling.

'You'll do no such ting. And you? You ought to be ashamed of yourself. Your mammy would be turning –'

'I tink we've already used that one.'

'Anyway, next time we see her in Bewley's –'

'– gout permitting –'

'– she'll be fully appraised, you mark our words.'

'And if she happens to choke to det on one of her beloved cream horns –'

'– then blame will be apportioned –'

'– at the appropriate door.'

The three aunts stood, as one, up to their full height.

'We rest our case.'

'For fuck's sake,' said JP. 'Fuck these fucken oul wans.'

The three aunts narrowed their eyes.

'And your name is?'

JP looked like a small boy caught woggling his willy. 'Benny,' he said sheepishly.

'No ih bleepin is noh,' said Benny. He looked pleadingly at the aunts. 'He's JP. *I'm* Benny. You meh Clemmie. And these is Pio, Inny, Grego, Zoz, Syl, Aido, Marty, Pauly an' Winston.'

The aunts listened attentively.

'Well, we're sure you're all very good boys deep down.'

JP continued to sulk. He wasn't lying down to this.

107

'Jesus,' he muttered. 'Leh's get the fuck owa heah. This is doin me fucken head in.' He turned to Frankie. 'Mind yor fucken ways yew. An remembah. We know where you live.' He stumbled off, followed by eleven squat Popes. '*Bleepin*, Benny?' he said as they disappeared down the hill. '*Bleepin?* I mean for fuck's sake. Thass an abuse a langwidge. Afraid of a few oul wans, hoh?'

'Well,' said Benny. 'Sorta, like, *yeh.*'

And they were gone.

21

Frankie Pope sat, head in hands, on the verge of the shallow grave. His bravado had fled with his brothers. He was now simply a young and broken man.

'You can't speak to those people,' he muttered.

Dottie, or perhaps Florrie, pulled her skirt up and removed a hip flask from her stocking. Hayden was beyond shocked. Frankie Pope as a woman he could take. But his nonagenarian aunts? Stockings? He may even have caught a glimpse of thigh. On the plus side, one stocking, one thigh, one aunt. It could have been six, six and three. Set against that, Eros had closed a very important door in his imagination, and it would probably stay closed forever. Truth to tell, it's beginning to have the same effect on me, so let's move discreetly on.

'Here you are, Francis. For medicinal purposes only.'

Frankie sighed and took a short swig, then sat for some minutes in silence. Eventually he looked up, weary-eyed, and took another swig.

'I didn't know Ma went to Bewley's,' he said.

The three aunts exchanged a glance.

'She didn't.'

'Oh look, girls. Butterflies.'

'They're not butterflies. They're those little things you get when your eyes go all wonky.'

Maybe it was the wisdom of age, the desire to leave the two young gentlemen alone, or maybe they genuinely collected those little things you get when your eyes go all wonky, but off they tripped through the bracken like spring lambs, wielding make-believe nets.

Hayden removed a pipistrelle bat from his hair and sat on a rock. Frankie Pope took another contemplative swig and sighed deeply.

'Lucky you lot were around,' he said. 'Picnic, was it?'

Hayden laughed. 'Not quite,' he said. 'Scattering the uncle's ashes.' He paused for a moment. 'Uncle Eddie,' he said. 'Eddie McGlynn.'

The effect was just as he expected.

'What? Eddie? As in…?'

'As in,' said Hayden. 'The very same.'

Frankie sighed again. 'A great man. A truly inspirational man.' Frankie mulled this over. Hayden felt the twinge he always felt when the subject of Eddie's greatness came up. The familial pride, and yet – something else. Something he tried to suppress.

'The thing is,' said Frankie, 'Your Uncle Eddie. He understood me.' He tapped the side of his head. 'He knew what was going on up here.'

Then it all came out. I won't go into detail because it's pretty much the experience of everyone led towards a life of crime by social forces beyond their control. Family. Class. Schooling. Interesting point on the secondary school front, though. I went to St. Aloysius of the Little Flower CBS[12], so did Frankie. I grew up in Clontarf, Frankie grew up in Killester. I was in the A class. Frankie? Straight into D. See? Social forces. He also happened to get landed with a violent mother, several absent fathers – they never found the bodies – and twelve violent brothers. So how come he alone, of all the brothers, got the brains? Different one of the several fathers is my guess, which would also explain Winston, but I wouldn't say that to his mother. Gout can turn a mean woman meaner. I just hope that if Big Mags ever comes across a book called *Sloot,* annotated or not, she opts to read something else. Otherwise, in the argot of the criminal class, I'm fucked.

---

[12] Name changed to protect the guilty.

Back to Frankie Pope. While I've been describing his background, Frankie has dealt with specifics:

- A spell in reform school, which is where he first met Eddie, who did some voluntary teaching and awakened Frankie's love of art.
- A couple of Open University degrees.
- Several spells in detention on behalf of his brothers, courtesy of Lou Brannigan.
- Shrewd investment in the art market, which enabled him to buy a detached house in Clontarf; re-meeting Eddie over the back wall when the latter was collecting windfalls for the latest batch of Sweet Ambrosia.

He'd just got to the bit where Eddie had convinced him to pose for *Portrait of a Lady* when –

'Coo-ee, Hayding.'

'Tree tirty-tree beckons.'

'Time to remove the urn from its receptacle –'

'– and spread Eddie while the moon is still up.'

'The mooooon.'

Rusty, who had been lying morosely in the bracken the whole time, sat up. His good ear twitched. He raised his face to the clear night sky.

'Owoooooooooooo.'

Hayden checked his watch. The time was tree tirty-one.

Hayden held the urn out, then hesitated. He felt a welling up of emotion. Love. Tenderness. Sorrow. An idolisation of sorts. And something he couldn't find a word for. Something not quite so loving. Something dark, brooding, clenched. But overriding everything, a deep sense of loss. He lifted the urn skyward, upended it and poured it out to join the elements. The gusting wind changed direction and blew his uncle's ashes back into his tear-stained face, over his coat, and across his still-damp trousers. Rusty, suddenly rejuvenated, barked noisily, stood next to Hayden and, as if obeying a summons from above, cocked an idle leg. Then he raced off down the hill, turning every few feet to yelp at Hayden to follow.

22

Hayden knew several car songs. *Three Little Aunts Sitting in the Front Seat* wasn't one of them. He sat silent in the back. Frankie Pope didn't know it either. *He* sat silent in the back. The pink 1963 Mini bounced down towards the city to the rhythm of the a cappella aunts. And then a curious thing happened. The aunts fell silent; their little heads stopped bobbing about. The car bounced on.

Hayden looked over at Frankie Pope, alleged godfather of crime. He sat hunched in his seat, a pair of reading glasses on the end of his nose, engrossed in what looked like a literary magazine by the light of the pre-dawn moon. Was it possible that this mild-mannered, ostensibly studious young man had killed Eddie? Had Lou Brannigan got Frankie Pope totally wrong? Hayden mulled this over: implications of.

I, meanwhile, was processing some new information of my own. I always thought I'd got into St. Al's top tier on merit, but if Frankie Pope was typical, I may have gained automatic entry based solely on my postcode. If I'd been aware of this at the time, it might have toned down the arrogance and assumption of superiority which I wore, lightly it has to be said, through my teens and early twenties, and made me a nicer person. Such is life. I am what I am. Enough.

The car seemed to glide through the pre-dawn city, smooth and silent as it crossed the Liffey and headed along the quays, down Amiens Street, past Fairview Park and my old alma mater, under the railway bridge and home, the only sound the gentle, triple-nosed snores wafting in tiny waves from the front seats.

The Mini pulled up outside Frankie Pope's security gate. A milk float trundled to a halt. The subject of a forthcoming documentary, *The Last Milkman in Christendom*, leapt out and placed a bottle by the gate. He hurried back to the float and trundled off to his next address twelve miles away.

Frankie Pope removed his spectacles, folded them neatly, placed them in his breast pocket and sighed.

'He won't deliver to the door,' he said. 'Thinks there's dogs and heavies and stuff in there. Fact is, I don't like heavies, and dogs pump up my histamine levels.' He ruffled Rusty's head before continuing. Rusty was apparently exempt. 'I don't even lock the security gate. Reputation, eh? If only they knew.'

He folded the journal and held it out to Hayden. 'Great piece about Clontarf in here,' he said. 'Might be of interest. Anyway, best be off. Oh, and I'm not a drinker, but if you ever fancy a coffee, we could always do Bewley's.' He grinned sheepishly. 'Preferably when the ma's not around.'

Hayden glanced over at Frankie as he pocketed the magazine. It's true what they say, he thought: we choose our enemies, but our mothers choose themselves.

The 1963 Mini is a two-door saloon. Frankie managed to prise his way past the one-and-a-half aunts snoring gently in the front passenger seat. He turned back at the gate, waved and was gone. The three aunts were now wide awake in the glorious moon-fading hour before dawn.

'Youse two behaved yourselves *very* well in the back, Hayding.'

Rusty barked his agreement.

'But it's been a busy night, and your old aunties are a bit long in the toot for this class of carry on.'

'So off you pop to beddy-byes like a good boy, and we'll see you on the morrow.'

Hayden stretched and yawned. 'I might just unwind a bit first,' he said. 'Listen to a couple of tapes.'

He regretted it as soon as he'd said it. *You don't tell your aunts anything they don't need to know.* Remember? They turned to face him like a three-headed hydra.

'Tapes, Hayding? So you *were* listening to them after all?'

'Well, sort of,' he stammered. 'You know. For educational purposes. They're... they're very... educational.' They stared at him, expecting him to go on, so he did. 'Fascinating social history and... stuff.'

Their eyes narrowed.

'We see, Hayding. We *see.*'

'So how far have you got?'

'With the... *stuff.*'

'Oh, you know. Not very far.' He fake-yawned for effect. 'Might just give them a miss. That's it. Straight to bed for me.'

'We see, Hayding. We *see.*'

Hayden thought about this as he walked up the driveway towards Eddie's front door, with Rusty trotting, I'm tempted to say trustily, by his side. *We see, Hayding, we see.* They'd said that twice, but he couldn't, despite giving the matter a good deal of earnest thought, see what it was that they saw.

I'm reminded of that clichéd old dictum 'I'll sleep when I'm dead', usually attributed to world record-holding insomniac Sleepy Zee. Hayden went for the amended version: I'll sleep when I'm in bed. Far more sensible. But first: he didn't know it yet, but Hayden was about to solve a case.

He dismissed the three aunts' little obsession with the tapes. Probably some 'adult' content they didn't want him to hear; he was, after all, only forty-three. Having said that, he'd gone off the idea of listening to them now. What if the aunts checked up on him? Instead, he unfolded Frankie Pope's magazine, *Intertextualities.* Frankie was certainly the deep one. Hayden flicked through the pages. Weighty stuff. Impenetrable poetry, impenetrable prose.[13] His head was starting to hurt. But hold on. Frankie had mentioned something about Clontarf. He speed-read the opening lines of each entry. Nothing to suggest – ah! Found it!

I should perhaps declare an interest here. I wrote the piece in question. I know, I know. Delusions of grandeur and all that. I've always had a hankering for a modicum of literary success. But never mind its intrinsic literary value; Hayden was soon more interested in the article's subject matter which is based, I might add, on a true story.

Here's an edited version. The full text will, of course, be available in the annotated *ibid*. But the essence:

> Clontarf was, compared to the rest of the
> country, a hotbed of multi-culturalism in the late
> fifties, by which I mean there was a foreigner
> living on Kincora Road. So unusual was this that
> a plaque was erected to mark the historic spot.
> We were never formally introduced but had a
> run-in anyway and here, in distilled form, is my
> side of the story.
>
> I was a very small boy, as was the fashion in
> those days, and nothing pleased me more than
> to wander from garden to garden in search of
> adventure. One day I must have strayed further
> than usual and found myself in a strange garden,
> littered – no pun where none intended – with
> dead felines. Curious. My child's mind was both
> repelled and fascinated. Just then I spotted
> an earnest-looking man of Germanic aspect
> shoving our family cat Houdini into a large box.
> Job done, he began scribbling furiously onto a
> nearby blackboard.

---

[13] 'Abstruse. Recondite. Recherché.' – PJ O'Malley

Undaunted, I stepped forward and, at the
precise point of his stentorian Germanic
'Eureka!', whipped the box open. As my hand
located Houdini, a dark shadow fell across
my line of vision. That's funny, I thought
precociously, that shadow doesn't belong to
the man. Unless he's working on light particle
displacement theory and has paused for a bit of
harmless fun.

As I yanked Houdini out of the box, a large
female hand fell over mine. I looked up. It was
accompanied by a large female.

'That is Herr Schrödinger's *Katze*, little boy,'
she said. 'And I think you've just killed it.'

Hayden closed the magazine. He located a black marker and
wrote *Ref. Schrödinger* in bold letters on the cover.

Verschiebung. The word springs back into play here. Hayden
had managed to relegate Marina from his frontal lobes by sheer
force of will; not always, but mainly. Sometimes his defences
fell and those frontal lobes were right in there, and they were
certainly right in there now. Having said that, this is not an
erotic novel, although I may have to reconsider as we approach
the – I hope – thrilling climax. Possible scene for the film
version: Marina, the flash of her eyes, the curve of her breast,
the rustle of silk...

Sorry. I've just had an unfortunate flashback.

Ref. Schrödinger. It seemed so – what's the word? – unfinished.
Hayden couldn't resist adding *Yours Sincerely, H* to the journal's
cover. He had his subliminal reasons.

He left Rusty tucking happily into a tin of Madden's Gold
Star Prawn Cocktail Brunch, slipped quietly out of the house
in the pre-dawn half-light, walked quickly down the driveway,
across the road, and up Marina's drive. He pushed the magazine
through the letterbox, listened for the thud on the mat, and

lowered the flap gently to stop it snapping shut. He had a moment of doubt. Perhaps he should have blacked out the title.

Intertextualities.

Would a woman like Marina open a magazine with such a title, let alone read it? Even with the *Ref* bit? And if she did, spurred on by natural curiosity, would she read the suggested piece? Erwin Schrödinger? Who, she might think, was Erwin Schrödinger, and why should she possibly be interested? But then she might see the cat reference and think 'A-*ha!*'

This was mere conjecture on Hayden's part. The magazine, and Marina's take on it, was now in the lap of the gods. He began to retrace his steps to Eddie's when he had a thought. The *Marina : Court* sign! Good time to check it out. He was sure it read *Courtesan*. Very Clontarf. But best to make sure. He grabbed hold of a rhododendron bough and was about to pull it away from the sign when a susurrating sound upset the early morning stillness. He glanced over at the three aunts' house, caressed by the waning but still bright moon. Behind the cotoneaster, also caressed, bobbed three wizened heads. He thought about saying 'It's not what you think', but 'It's not what you think' usually means 'It's exactly what you think', which in this case it wasn't, so he opted for a not-a-care-in-the-world whistle and strode, faux-nonchalant, back to Eddie's.

He sat with the headphones on, the living room discreetly lit by a dusty lamp, gazing out on the back garden, and pressed Play. A quick dose of displacement therapy and off to bed. It might be noted at this point that he'd totally forgotten about finding Eddie's killer. I find myself wondering if this book might be better suited to the literature section. But this is to pre-empt, not to mention digress, which you simply don't do under Crime.

The tape he'd chosen was *Suffer Little Chizzlers*. Chizzlers is a charming Dublin expression which features in the *Oxford English Dictionary* as 'No Entries Found'. Their loss. The tape in question certainly made a nice change from Eddie's more artistic offerings. A small boy chortling with delight as Eddie showed him some of his more playful artworks. Example: A Dublin Underground with all the stations marked out on the floor and, under the floorboards, the sound of the Circle Line passing through Tallaght. As Hayden listened to the tape, the memories flooded back, the years fell away. Then this:

EDDIE: Someday you'll be a great artist just like –

Hayden turned the tape off, overcome by a sudden and profound sadness. He sat and thought about the small boy he once was. He thought about Eddie and yes, Eddie was a great artist. Way ahead of his time. And Hayden? He thought about all the artistic compromises he'd made over the years. *Only Quotin'*: a dreadful TV quiz show with seemingly obligatory swearing.[14] *Father Brown's Boys*: 'The paedophile priest thingy.' Sadly, however, they weren't the nadir of an otherwise creditable career. Hayden had been on the way up, much like Foetus O'Flaherty. He'd just signed up with hot comedy agent Richard Mann. Hayden was offered an Irish Tourist Board ad.

'Whatever it takes, mate,' Rich had drawled.

Hayden whatever-it-tooked. Toadstool. Leprechaun suit. Ignominy. And now he sat with his head in his hands and wept for his tragically compromised past. Pretty standard procedure for those of a comic bent, to be honest. Angst? Don't talk to me about angst.

Having said that, the leprechaun suit ad was particularly bad. So, head in hands, salt tears.

Hayden had been up all night. I too. But Hayden had been on an emotional rollercoaster, while I'd merely been taking notes. He made up the sofa, and was about to plump up the cushions when Rusty barked furiously and raced out into the hall. Hayden followed him, yawning.

---

[14] Aren't we Irish *terrible*?

'What is it, Rusty?' he said.

Rusty barked a response. He was now standing outside the door to Hayden's childhood bedroom. Maybe, thought Hayden, he's seen a mouse. Plausible. There was a gap under the door. But this wasn't just any door. Hayden's childhood was in there. His hopes, his dreams, his hurt – which is why he slept on the sofa. His head was a mass of warring emotions. He stood frozen for a long moment, then steeled himself and opened the door to the width of a small dog. Rusty raced in, still barking. Hayden stood outside and waited. Silence.

'Come on, old son,' yawned Hayden. 'Bedtime.'

No response. Hayden walked away. He stood by the living room door and waited. Repeated the request. Still no response. He sighed and plodded wearily back to the bedroom door. What was it with aunts and dogs?

'Rusty,' he said. 'Out. Now.'

Nothing. Not a sound. Probably playing a game, thought Hayden, but he really wasn't in the mood. Poor old Rusty, though. Is a bit of harmless fun with your new best pal too much to ask? Put like that he would have to say no, so he forced himself to face up to his demons and dragged himself wearily in. Put the light on. Stood there, all thoughts of sleep momentarily gone. The room was exactly as it was when he was little. He'd spent most of his teen years here as well, but Eddie had re-decorated it exactly as it had been when he was seven – and what a revelation to his adult eye.

The lights were a riot of tiny pinpoints, dotted into the ceiling like multi-coloured stars; the Plough and the Milky Way jumbled together in a crazy, playful pattern. Shelves lined the far wall, stacked with Eddie-made, Hayden-friendly toys. The duvet cover was a young Hayden woven abstractly into the fabric, hands behind his head, looking dreamily up at the night sky.

Hayden was suddenly overcome with an exhaustion he couldn't fight. He rubbed his eyes and leaned heavily on a small desk by the window, a scaled-down replica of Eddie's desk downstairs. On top of it, slightly incongruously, sat a thick brown folder, but Hayden was too tired to notice. He yanked himself away from the desk with a groan and flopped down on the bed. He thought of Eddie, re-imagining his room long after Hayden had grown up and gone away, and it filled him with sadness, longing and regret.

He thought he heard a noise in the living room. Yes. There was no doubt about it. Three tiny voices. Six tiny feet. Why? What could they possibly be doing here at this time in the morning? But he was tired. So, so tired. He curled up on top of the duvet like the child he'd once been, and never would be again. As soon as he fell asleep, Rusty re-appeared from under the bed, hopped up beside Hayden and snuggled contentedly in.

There never had been a mouse.

23

E arly morning. Beautiful day. I was gazing out the front
window, wondering how best to occupy myself while Hayden
slept the sleep of the innocent, when the learned Professor flew
past on his bicycle. Perfect! I left Hayden to his much-needed
sleep, raced outside, grabbed hold of Eddie's bike and gave
chase. A quick internet search had established that there was
no such place as UDC; I'd also established that he wasn't known
at CDU, so where exactly was he headed? Professor Emeritus
Stern was my guru. I'd applied his comic theories to my own
work – indeed *life* – for years, yet he seemed to exist, at some
level, outside what is often referred to as the real world. Where
exactly? I had to find out. My mental equilibrium demanded it.

Stern, his magnificent white head backlit by the early morning
sun, was easy enough to follow, and he seemed to be heading in
the general direction of CDU and the formidable Áine. I wasn't
looking forward to meeting her again. Her response to my initial
enquiry had been terse in the extreme. No such person. No such
facility. No bicycles in reception. But perhaps, apart from the
bike bit, she'd got it wrong. Perhaps the Department of Comedic
Arts was housed in a separate building, outside her adminis-
trative jurisdiction. Only one way to find out.

I dropped the pressure on Eddie's pedals and kept a safe
distance. I began to see myself in the romantic role of the
accidental detective, a gumshoe for the modern age. No harm if
Stern spotted me, I supposed. He was hardly likely to beat me to
a pulp if he caught me. Not physically anyway; possibly intellec-
tually, but I was more worried about my face. I pedalled on, lost
in accidental detective thoughts of cigarettes and bourbon and

dames, and the thing dames always bring: trouble. It's hard to escape that golden era of noir when you're lost in fantasy land, even when you're panting up Castle Avenue on a superannuated two-wheeler with dodgy gears.

I came back from fantasy land. Damn. While I'd been dawdling, the Professor had almost reached the top of Castle Avenue. He mounted the pavement, put on a sudden burst of speed I wouldn't have thought possible in a man of his age, and turned left up Howth Road. I shifted up a rusted gear, pedalled as fast as the rickety bike allowed, and turned left myself. No sign of him. Perhaps he'd turned right into Collins Avenue? I did likewise; still no sign. I arrived at the hallowed entrance to CDU. The learned Professor had totally disappeared. I turned back, cursing myself for that momentary lapse in concentration.

Dames, huh?

Hayden woke at midday to find himself staring at the ceiling of his childhood bedroom. It seemed less unsettling in daylight, so he shifted Rusty off the duvet and tumbled out of bed. He now realised that Eddie, in his own undemonstrative way, had loved him. Eddie had given him a home. Eddie had believed he could be a great artist. He'd even preserved his childhood room as a shrine. But Hayden had failed him – until now. Maybe he wasn't a sloot. Maybe he wasn't cut out to be a detective. But he could write a great detective novel. Make Eddie proud. He had the time, he had the place. All he needed was the inspiration. He'd worked his way through Bram's charity shop box, so why not pop in to Eason's, see what sort of stuff was selling? Fact. Fiction. Whatever. Another lovely day, so the walk would do him good.

A quick pot of tea later, he marched down the driveway in a positive frame of mind. Kincora Road was abuzz with activity. *Intertextualities* had borne fruit. The Schrödinger house was cordoned off. Garda cars with lights flashing. A sizeable crowd of onlookers. Detective Inspector Lou Brannigan pacing about, his trilby cocked at a jaunty angle. This was a cop in control.

He was onto something, and Hayden knew what it was. He was passing on his way into town anyway, so he sauntered over to the scene of the crime.

The three aunts were already there.

'Isn't that gas, Hayding? Our young friend in there has been bumping off moggies and burying them out the back.'

'It's all to do with Herr Schrödinger. Our young friend's an acolyte, apparently.'

'Aren't we all? Disciple, votary, call it what you will. I mean, Herrdinger's ground-breaking experiments in teoretical physics have been called into question in the light of subsequent discoveries about alternative universities and so on –'

'– but what a lover! No question there.'

'He's welcome trew our cat flap any time.'

Hayden wasn't listening. A pale-faced young man with a wispy moustache and matching three-piece tweed was being escorted from the premises by a couple of gardaí. Cameras flashing. The usual media scrum. Lou Brannigan eased the subject's head down in a self-important way and manoeuvred him into the back of the squad car. He closed the door, fanned himself with the trilby and placed it back on his head, jaunty angle intact. Hayden coughed politely.

'Ah, 'tis yourself.' Brannigan kept up the pretence for the cameras, but behind the eyes was a chastened look.

'It wasn't Rusty then,' said Hayden with a hint of told-you-so.

'Yerr, I suppose we may well close the book on that one.'

Behind the badge of office, the public show and the satisfaction of a case which had seemingly solved itself, Brannigan was deeply, deeply ashamed, and there was a reason for his shame. This case was Brannigan's very own *Verschiebung*. But we'll get to that.

For myself, I'm glad it's resolved. The whole thing was a bit daft, to be honest, and I can't think that anyone bought Brannigan's ridiculous theory about Rusty in the first place.

24

I love the walk into town myself. A quiet stroll down Castle Avenue to the sea front. Along the promenade to Marino and Fairview park. You then have a choice of route. Straight on to the city centre via the Five Lamps, turn right up Talbot Street just past Amiens Street station, Dinny Guiney's on the left, on to O'Connell Street, cross at the faux-Eddie statue, left past the GPO and there's your bookshop.

Or hang a right to sunny Summerhill.

Hayden chose the Summerhill option, which brings you deep into the heart of the city from a different angle. He was in excellent spirits. Whistling internally, playing with possible opening lines for his book, when the sound of gunfire cut across the hum of inner-city traffic.

Crack!

The doors of Sunshine House, a corner pub with blacked-out windows, flew open, and out stormed several men in balaclavas. Stocky men. Pope-shaped.

'You seen nuhhin,' barked one, as shocked pedestrians fled in all directions. He stopped and turned to Hayden as he passed.

'How's the bewke comin, maestro?'

The man behind him whipped him over the balaclava with a pistol butt. 'Jayz, Benny, yor supposed ta be ingogneeho. Will ya fucken come *on* for fuck's sake.'

A car screamed around the corner. Benny turned to Hayden as he ducked to get in.

'We're the good guys, righ?' he roared. 'Or fucken else.'

And off they sped, with sirens wailing in the distance. This was serious, and pretty soon all that remained of the screen-play-friendly scene was a long line of Garda cars, police tape, and Lou Brannigan, fanning himself with his sweat-damp trilby and trudging into the darkened pub.

Hayden was pretty shaken up when he arrived at Eason's, but he was also relieved. He'd seen nuhhin. Actually, that wasn't strictly true. He'd given Brannigan a statement. It was, definitively and unarguably, the Popes. Not that it mattered, because Brannigan wasn't listening. He knew it was the Popes. With Lou Brannigan, it was always the Popes and this time, for once, he was right.

But Eason's. Hayden headed straight for Crime. Now this was interesting. Quilty, the criminal pathologist from the Nautical Buoy, had written a book: *Quilty as Charged.* Good title. Flattering photo on the front cover, although to be fair he was a pretty good-looking man in the flesh and, according to the back flap, 'Dublin's Hottest Pathologist'. Hayden was intrigued. He flicked to the opening page.

'I woke with a thudding head.'

Good opener. Not surprising, frankly, given how much he drank, but it drew you in. Unfortunately, the next fourteen pages dwelt lovingly, almost pornographically to Hayden's mind, on the late morning sunlight slanting through the dust-mite-darkened bedroom curtains. Odd way to start your autobiography. Hayden was about to flick further on when he became aware of a woman tutting next to him, the shoplifter-repellent lights accentuating her sharp features and disapproving nose.

'It's no wonder bookshops are going out of business,' she sneered, prising the book from him and returning it, sniffily, to the shelf. Hayden held his hands up. Quilty as charged! He pottered about for a while longer, but the sense of her unforgiving eyes boring into the small of his back ruined any enjoyment he might have got from a casual browse.

Outside, he noticed, there was a ten-cent table. Books that hadn't made it to the cash register. He glanced up. The assistant had taken her judgemental face elsewhere. He rummaged through the books.

'An elegiac masterpiece' – *The Guardian*

'A bona-fide masterpiece' – *The Guardian*

'A luminous masterpiece' – *The Guardian*

'Quite simply a masterpiece' – *The Guardian*

Difficult to tell why they were on the ten-cent table with endorsements like those, but that's the modern world for you. Maybe people have just lost their appetite for masterpieces.

Ah. This was more like it. Lou Brannigan's all-time favourite, *Holy Joe*. A snip at the markdown, thought Hayden. He picked it up and had just started flicking through its action-packed pages when he was prodded by a reproving finger. The assistant, seemingly alert to his every move, was back. Hayden rooted in his pocket and produced some loose change.

'There you are, my good woman,' he said. 'No bag required.'

It may have been that she was unused to being called a good woman, but the assistant's mood changed. Her features softened. Her nose lost its disapproving look and returned to what may well have been its natural state: aquiline. Hayden pocketed the book. The assistant pocketed the money. I say assistant. She didn't actually work there but that, along with the hyperbolic book reviews, is also the modern world.

Hayden, fortunately for him, had other things to think about as he made his way back to the bus stop, so he missed this. He also missed the crowd gathered outside the shop window filled with TV screens, not to mention their ecstatic call and response.

'Hey fella, where you from?'

'Termonfeckin!'

'Yow!'

At the Abbey Street terminal the bus sat ready to depart. Directly opposite Ireland's National Theatre, which was devoted to addressing an alleged gender imbalance with a season devoted exclusively to male writers. Hayden made a mental note and leapt on board. The driver? Bram. And he was in bus driver mode.

'Sorry, Haydo, but it's exact fare only. I'd pay it myself but you know how it is. Where would it all end? Preferential treatment, you know?'

Hayden pressed a five euro note furiously into the slot. That, he thought, was some markup, but what could you do? Bram tapped his forehead, started the engine and pulled out. Hayden held a copy of *Holy Joe* up to the glass and was about to ask Bram if he'd read it, but Bram cut him short. He pointed primly to the no-talking-to-the-driver-while-the-bus-is-in-motion sign. Hayden exhaled meaningfully and moved up the aisle in search of a seat.

Pascal O'Dea was sitting on his own, the vacant seat beside him the only one on offer. Hayden sat down. No hint of recognition.

'I killed my own daddy,' said Pascal, 'with the belt of a loy.'

Hayden made a mental note to check out the Abbey's all-male *Playboy*.

'Of course you did, Pascal,' he intoned. 'Of course you did.'

He opened *Holy Joe*[15] and zoned out.

Here's the story in miniature. Dublin. The 1970s. Father Johnny Cracken's entry under hobbies in *Catholic Who's Who*: Aytin. Drinkin. Shaggin the housekeeper. He's a rogue and a wild one, but the more he tells the truth, the more people laugh: 'You're cracken me up, Father.' Orphans left on the church doorstep? They're all, according to him, the fruit of his priestly loins! Other examples? Read the book. But there's one person who's not amused, because Father Johnny dies a slow and painful death when a duty-free box of Capstan Full Strength mysteriously appears in his drinks cupboard. Laced with strychnine. Father Johnny Cracken RIP.

---

[15] 'A noir masterpiece' – *The Guardian*

I'll leave it there for now. The denouement is responsible for Hayden's big breakthrough. Don't want to give it away. But Hayden was riveted; so riveted, in fact, that he almost missed his stop. The plan was to get off at the Nautical Buoy and speed-read the book to its tragic conclusion over a cold drink and, luckily for him, Pascal stood up timidly. Pascal's stop, Hayden's stop too. Pascal was chattering away, something about Martin Luther King, but Hayden continued reading and missed out on the solution to one of the iconic murders of the mid-twentieth century. His head buried in *Holy Joe*'s penultimate chapter, he felt his way up to the front of the bus.

'What's the book?' Bram said, as he pulled over to the stop.

Hayden pointed absently at the no-talking sign. The doors swung open and Hayden and Pascal got off. Pascal had now moved on to Julius Caesar[16], but Hayden didn't catch his eyewitness update on a shameful miscarriage of justice. His head was still stuck in the book.

---

[16] *'Et tu, Pascal?'*

25

The lunchtime specials, if Voot O'Rooney's laid-back jazz was to be believed, were *Crayfish Salad & Melon Meringue*. They weren't. Nice rhythm, though.

Hayden took a seat and waited for table service. The Nautical Buoy didn't do table service, but he didn't mind waiting. He was deeply engrossed in the plot twists and turns of *Holy Joe* as it reached its heart-rending finale. Fiendishly clever stuff. I'll be the first to admit that *Sloot* has no such twists and turns. Or am I being unnecessarily humble?

One thing about *Holy Joe*, though. The narrator doesn't continually interrupt himself with lengthy asides on subjects as diverse as the nature of comedy, the healing properties of Assam, and the merits and demerits of the book in question as literature on the one hand, crime thriller on the other. Valuable lesson there if I decide to stick to genre fiction for my next outing. Bit late for this one, though.

Holy Joe hit the home stretch in taut, lean prose. One-syllable words, apart from 'guilty' and 'mother'. Shorty Sminks was flummoxed. Shorty, as pulp aficionados will doubtless know, is an orphan detective with a speech impediment, two club feet and a rejection letter from the Harlem Globetrotters simply because he isn't black. The speech impediment, and this may upset certain readers, is a Limerick accent, and boy! This is one case he wishes he hadn't taken on! Shorty is, as I say, floundering, so – and here's where Hayden took note – he calls everyone together for the classic perp-is-in-this-very-room denouement. But here's the twist: Shorty hasn't a clue who the guilty party is, so he counts them off one by one. The Parish Priest.

Check. The local tobacconist. Check. The deceased reprobate's housekeeper and four of his 'waifs and strays'. To wit, the fruit of his aforementioned loins disguised as homeless orphans left on the also aforementioned doorstep. Fathered by Father Johnny. Mothered, as it turns out, by several housekeepers. Check. Here's where the breakthrough comes.

No sooner has he established the pitiful housekeepers' collective innocence than the only person left in the room cracks. The late departed cleric's beloved mother! Her son is a priest. She's the only woman in his life. Except she isn't! She's sharing him, it seems, with half the housekeepers in Dublin. Worse. All those little orphans and not one of them hers! Which explains the tagline: 'Mother love is a two-way street.' Case solved. She's dragged off to a life of penal servitude but hangs herself in the non-gender-specific prison lavatory with a skilfully removed thread of Dinny Guiney's reinforced corset elastic.[17]

Hayden finished the book with the curiously empty feeling you get when you find out who perped it. It all seems a bit obvious in the end. The mother. Of course. Who else? He smiled wanly at the predictability of it all. Then it hit him: he'd do the same for Eddie's killer! Hold a memorial bash for Eddie. Invite the suspects. Flush the perp out. Because the perp was sure to come. They always did.

He tossed *Holy Joe* on the table and returned from the fictional world of 1970s Ireland to the lounge of the Nautical Buoy. The place had been filling up. Quilty, Dublin's hottest pathologist, stood beneath the skylight in meditative mood. A shaft of sunlight refracted off his tumbler at an obtuse angle. He drained the glass and swayed unsteadily to the counter. The shaft followed him over, the angle decreasing to acute as he approached his goal.

---

[17] 'Cherchez la maman,' raved *Le Monde*. 'Très irlandais.'

He slapped the empty glass down. 'A double helping of your finest Isle of Ulay single malt, my dear, and a little of what you fancy for your exquisitely lovely self.'

Declan closed the till and turned to face him. 'Don't you think you may have had enough, Mr Q?'

Quilty, crestfallen, caressed his glass like a comfort blanket, and in his sorrowful expression Hayden saw his chance.

Quilty swayed unsteadily on the pavement outside the Nautical Buoy as he waved his empty glass at a passing cab. The cab swerved and turned.

'It's less than a ten-minute walk,' protested Hayden, but Quilty was already pouring himself into the back seat. Hayden, overruled by Quilty's alcohol intake, opened the other door. Quilty squeezed the cab driver's shoulder affectionately.

'Home, James,' he slurred, 'and spare not the horses.'

The driver winked at Hayden through the rear-view mirror. 'Any advance on thah?' He switched his gaze to Quilty. 'Dryin ouh clinic, is ih?'

Should be, but wasn't. Hayden almost laughed. 'The opposite,' he said. 'I promised him a top-up.'

'Fair enough,' said the taxi driver. 'If I was thah way inclined, I'd fancy him meself.'

Hayden left it there. You never knew where these things might lead. Besides, he had other plans for Quilty. If he wanted to establish beyond reasonable doubt that Eddie had been murdered, Quilty was the man to do it, and there was no way he was going any further down the single malt alphabet at the Nautical Buoy in his present condition. He'd lured Quilty on the promise of Eddie's generous stock of Scotland's finest A to Zs. He gave the cabbie Eddie's address in a gruff manner intended to close the conversation down, but the driver was in talkative mood.

'You'll never guess who I had in the cab las nigh. The wife's cousin Lorelei. See? Ih's noh all pop stars, fillum stars an world fucken leaders. Off to the airport she was. Didn charge her a course. The wife'd a killed me.' He wiped an eye and may have sniffled quietly. 'Still feel a bih guilty abouh her fella. Two bulleh job. Finglas. Wha a way to go, you know? Last thing you see. Finglas.' He reached a stubby hand over the back. 'Grego Pope, by the way, on'y I seen you up the hills the other nigh. Lovely spoh.' Hayden shook the hand. It seemed, on balance, the safest bet. 'Thing is, there's no point takin thah shallow grave stuff too serious. Sure those lads is all bluster. Well, aparh from the hold ups an the gang feuds an the savage internecine warfare. Righ, thass you here. Four euros eigh'y. To be honest, there's more money in bank jobs. Thass the wife's take, anyway.' He glanced at the meter and set it back at nought. 'She migh be righ abouh thah.'

'Await my imminent return, my estimable if unlovely friend,' slurred Quilty, as he worked out the mechanics of the door handle. 'Busy day, busy day.'

Hayden fumbled for a note. The driver nodded towards Quilty, who swayed gently up the drive, empty glass in hand. 'Isn't yor man someone?'

Hayden passed a five euro note to Grego and waved away the change. He got out, closed the door and leaned in at the driver's open window.

'In the broadest meaning of the term,' he said, 'I suspect he probably is.'

Quilty had now reached Eddie's front door, supporting himself precariously on his glass. The relationship seemed somehow symbiotic. Hayden followed and they went inside. That was the easy bit. Getting Quilty to switch to Uncle Eddie's Sweet Ambrosia might be a different matter; Hayden had lied about the single malt. He yanked the cork from the bottle and held it out.

'Not sure I'm best advised to drink that, old fruit,' said Quilty, thrusting his glass out eagerly. 'Bit out of character for a single malt man. Not, as it were, *me.*' He took a quick slurp nonetheless. 'Hmn. Interesting notes. Hint of –'

'Apple?' said Hayden, who wanted to get on. 'Sweet Ambrosia. It's a local brew.'

'Just so,' said Quilty. 'Sweet Ambrosia. Hmnn. Sherlock's sister, unless I'm much mistaken. Could add a whole new dimension to my – tell you what. Worth a try.' He held his glass out for a top-up. Hayden obliged. Quilty then swayed around the room, fingering the worktop for dust, peering into the teapot, and generally looking for clues, which wasn't much help to Hayden. He hadn't told him what the crime was yet. Quilty swayed over to Eddie's desk and ran his fingers along the tape boxes as if they were piano keys.

'Missing tape,' he slurred. 'Could mean something, could mean nothing.'

Hayden hadn't noticed it before, but now was not the time. He was beginning to regret his decision to ask Quilty over in the first place. He seemed to be ambling around the room mumbling nonsense. Hayden slammed the cork into the bottle and crossed to the cellar door. He pulled it open and flicked the light on.

'Here's the scene of Eddie's final moments,' he said. 'And this,' – he held his mobile out – 'is Eddie post mortem. Thoughts?'

Quilty reeled over, topped-up glass in hand, and bowed over the mobile. He then teetered alarmingly over the drop to the cellar before bending back over the phone. He stopped teetering and bending as if sobering up momentarily.

'Ah,' he said. 'Contusions to the left vertebrae suggest a mallet dropped from a great height. Or similar. So where might we find the deceased?'

'Cremated,' said Hayden.

Quilty stroked his chin with his free hand. 'Quinteresting,' he said. 'Most, most quinteresting. We could, one supposes, reassemble the corpse from his ashes for a closer look. And now' – he jerked his watch free of his sleeve – 'I really must get on. Busy day. Busy day.' He drained his glass and held it out for a refill; Hayden retrieved the bottle and slopped more liquid in. Quilty took a quick slurp and moved towards the door. 'Sweet Ambrosia of the Gods,' he said as Hayden ushered him out of the house. 'Could be the very thing. Slight change of emphasis. Younger image. Yes indeed. Could be the very thing.' His brow furrowed in concentration. 'Or, and this would be an interesting departure for my next outing, embrace sobriety. Thoughts?'

Hayden hadn't a clue what he was on about, so he held his own counsel as Quilty reeled down the driveway and hailed the stationary cab. He clambered in beside the driver, the cab did a quick u-turn and they were off. Hayden closed the door and ruffled Rusty's head. What a waste of time that had been.

Or had it? The missing tape. Hayden hadn't noticed it before. He noticed it now. *Could mean something, could mean nothing.* He filed it away for future reference. Quilty's seeming gibberish also contained within it an interesting clue as to his character, or rather his identity, which comes into play later. Page one-nine-three if you can't wait, but it really spoils the build-up. Besides, Hayden knows nothing about it until the page in question, and neither, for the purposes of sticking to the quasi-linear Inquisitive Bullet narrative, do I.

Hayden set about applying the lesson of *Holy Joe* to the next stage in his real life murder investigation. I won't go into detail, but all interested parties were contacted, including an email invite to his parents, who declined – and not, I might add, very graciously. Bad blood was hinted at. We're staying right where we are thank-you-very-much.

I'll draw an authorial veil over the melancholy twinge Hayden felt at their frankly dismissive tone. Okay, he was a man in his forties and he hadn't seen them since he was one day short of seven, but that was hardly the point. Your parents were your parents and they were supposed to love you, but not so much as an 'xxx'. He sighed and pressed Delete.

'I *have* no parents.' He didn't pout as he said it, but he would have if they'd been there, and then he would have left the room with a flounce. Rusty, who sat quietly at Hayden's feet, nuzzled in close. He may have been a mongrel of no fixed parentage, but *he* certainly wasn't lacking the empathy gene.

It made sense to hand-deliver the three aunts' invitation. The old fashioned way. He crept across the road late at night; he didn't want to get into one of those long, convoluted conversations that have been such a feature of the narrative thus far. He toyed with the idea of excluding them from the general invite, but no. They were, incontrovertibly, not on the same wavelength as other mortals. Tuned, if you will, to a different dimension, but that could work to his advantage. The sheer lunacy of their particular channel, to risk labouring the radio metaphor, might help flush the guilty party out.

He wanted them there. He wanted action. He wanted the perp banged up. Eddie deserved, nay, *demanded,* justice. He was about to ease the invitation through their polished brass letterbox when the door opened.

'Howaya, Hayding.'

'We seen you coming over.'

'On tippytoe.'

'Very consideracious, Hayding. We could have been asleep.'

'Except we weren't. We were looking out the window.'

'All tinking the same ting. We wonder what Hayding is up to all on his ownio over there.'

'And here you are, as if to answer our question in your very own words.'

'Would it, perchance, involve this envinglope?'

Hayden passed it over and explained his farewell-to-Eddie idea in as few words as possible, interrupted by several 'That's beautiful, Hayding's and 'What a toughtful boy you really are's.

'We can wear our Bewley's uniforms.'

'Which haven't been used since the late fifties.'

'Outside the bedroom anyway.'

'We can help out.'

'We've even got a spare one for your lovely lady.'

Hayden bridled. 'What lovely lady? I don't have a lovely lady.'

'Oh now, Hayding. No need to be coy. She uprooted from Londing to be closer to the object of her heart's desire.'

'As you well know.'

'So putting her up was the least we could do in her straitened circumstances.'

'The lowly checkout girl being woefully undervalued in dese neo-liberal times, Hayding.'

'But enough of revolutionary political teory.'

They turned their heads as one and yelled back into the house.

'Hear that? You're invited to a do.'

They turned back.

'We don't tink she can hear, Hayding.'

'She's having a quick soak in the baignoire.'

'We'll pass the message on.'

No point arguing with the aunts. Hayden should have left it at that, but he was annoyed. How could they have the gall to give succour, not to mention board and probably lodging, not also to mention baignoire, to his stalker?

He shouldn't have said the following, but he did. He should have stuck to the pretence that the invitation was for a celebratory farewell to Eddie, but he didn't. 'The fact is,' he said, 'I've set up the whole thing to flush out Eddie's killer.'

The aunts seemed to shrink into themselves, heads retracted like tortoises sensing peril.

'Is that so?'

'We see.'

They normally operated on the rule of three, but not this time. They fell silent. A silence that followed Hayden as he walked down their drive, past the cotoneaster, across the road, up Eddie's gravel drive and into Eddie's house. He closed and locked the door. Too late. The silence had followed him in.

26

Hayden was a busy man. The invites were out. He looked up 'baignoire' and found out what it meant. He went back over his plan. Several times. Without Bram. Big help. He also splashed out on some fizzy water. Oh, and nuts. Nothing else to be done, so he sat back and let the invitations do their work. Three days later –

But before that...

27

My own aversion to golf is well documented elsewhere. Hayden, in his defence, hated the so-called sport too, but the fact that he agreed to meet Bram for 'a quick round' tells its own story. A sentimental attachment to childhood friendship? Let's be charitable here. He lost by the odd hole in three – well, something along those lines – and accused Bram of switching his balls in the rough. But that's by the by. The important point is that I was to be cast adrift from my own novel for the duration. I had no intention of monitoring their progress in case one of them said something of interest. They were hardly likely to; this, after all, being golf.

I was outside Eddie's pondering my options – and savouring the smell of freshly mown grass, the tang of the sea, the glorious late June sunlight, the temporary absence of my main character – when the learned Professor flew past, his white hair dancing crazily in the breeze. I had to think quickly. How long is a game of golf? Would I manage to solve the CDU conundrum if I set off in hot pursuit immediately? This may be one of those mysteries – did Stern disappear from the leafy suburb of Clontarf into another dimension and, if so, how could I possibly find out? – of more interest to me than to others, plus it was a beautiful day, there was a break in the narrative, and – golf?

My mind was made up. I hurried around the side of the house and grabbed hold of Eddie's bike. I wheeled it quickly down the gravel driveway and hopped on. The ageing tyres had already gone a bit soft. No Pascal, no pump. Still, bit late to do anything about that now, so I redistributed my weight to minimise the effect and set off.

I raced along Kincora Road like a man possessed. I *was* a man possessed. I'd become convinced that Professor Stern, in pursuit of the comic afflatus, had entered a parallel universe. Was I right? I was also convinced that this would be my last chance to find out. I turned up Castle Avenue.

In the far distance, an eruption of white hair anointed by the sun. Grunt, grunt, grunt. The grunts were me, by the way. Stern, probably also grunting, mounted the pavement and turned left onto Howth Road. So did I but not, I hasten to add, on the pavement. No sign of the Professor up ahead. No beacon of white hair to light the way. No – but wait: a man in a bobble hat was pushing a bicycle through a house gate up ahead. Something about his movements alerted me. He looked like the Professor without the electrified hair; the hat would explain that. I raced on, got to the house, then – nothing. Not a sign. The front door opened. A different man came out, blinking into the sunlight. He looked around, puzzled. Scratched his head. Shook it. Went back in. Still puzzled. Inference? He thought he'd seen something, but his eyes had been deceiving him. Ah well. Back to daytime telly. Back, for me, to the Professor.

His bobble hat was the perfect disguise. Without the trademark mane, he looked like any other eccentric male cyclist of advancing years. But what about the rest of it? Why had he ducked into this particular house? Did he spend the day in a stranger's garage? Hardly. It was then that I noticed a narrow passage between the garage and the next-door-neighbour's wall. I decided to check it out and walked briskly up the driveway and along the passage, which led to a small, neatly-tended garden. At the far end was a modest fence backing onto the garden opposite, which was, seemingly, a mirror image of this one. Garden with garage, passageway leading to – aha! Easy enough to lift your bike over the fence, through the mirror image in reverse, out the front gate of the house opposite at – where exactly?

I raced back to Eddie's bicycle. Still there. I hopped on and raced back the way I'd come. I thought about mounting the pavement. Very anti-social I know, but I was a driven man on an ancient bicycle in the grip of an obsession. Normal rules of civilised behaviour didn't apply. Having said that, I didn't mount the pavement. I did, however, cycle on the wrong side of the road. I pedalled frantically till I reached the turn off to Castle Avenue, careered downhill and took the first available right which was, presumably, the street of the house opposite. From here, it was guesswork. The Professor had long since gone.

I had to make a snap decision with very little information to go on. Well, just one thing. Mirror image. That was my clue. I decided that the Professor, for reasons I couldn't begin to fathom, had decided to retrace his steps by a circuitous route. I raced along Stiles Road, through the stiles to Castle Avenue, and was about to speed down to Kincora Road when I thought, no, he wouldn't retrace his journey back along the same road. Think circuitous. Seafield Road. It had to be Seafield Road. Long shot, but it was the only shot I had.

I sped along Seafield Road, examining the houses to left and right. Big driveways. Secluded gardens. Impressive habitations. Nice if you could afford one. But as for locating the Professor, a pretty impossible task without a huge dose of luck. I was about to reconsider my options when my eyes were drawn to a slightly crazed figure at an upstairs window pulling off a woolly hat, releasing a magnificent head of white hair. I braked violently. There was my dose of luck.

A large sign, just inside the main gate:

HARDY LAING
ESTATE AGENTS

AND DAY CENTRE FOR THE TERMINALLY INSANE

I cycled up the long driveway, shaded by a grove of deciduous trees, parked Eddie's bicycle, and went in. Nobody about. Not a sound. Then –

'SILENCE!!!'

A huge man with flaming red hair and wing commander eyebrows marched into the vestibule. 'Sorry about that,' he roared. 'It's Bedlam in here!' He strode over to where I cowered at the entrance. 'Hardy Laing, Doctor of Lunacy,' he bellowed in a refined Scottish accent, Edinburgh South if I'm not mistaken. 'I was lumbered with an estate agent's name – it seemed churlish not to succumb to the lure of a quick semi-legal buck – but *insanity is my passion!* So, what brings *you* here?' He glanced down at my socks, still tucked over my trousers. 'Surprise me!'

A nurse led a patient out of a side door and along the corridor. Hardy Laing leaned in for a conspiratorial bellow. 'Napoleon. Sad case. He's convinced he's Declan Mulholland of 42b, Dunseverick Road, D3. I mean, *why?* Think of all he could have achieved as *himself!*' He leaned in closer. 'Now,' he enquired, producing a large syringe from his left trouser pocket, 'what seems to be the problem? And if it's aboot a hoose, *I won't accept a red cent under 12 million!*' He may have been about to leap on me with the syringe when he spotted something along the corridor. 'Nurse!' he roared. 'Put that man down. There's such a thing as a code of ethics.' He squirted the syringe at the ceiling and winked. Lewdly? Probably not, but it looked pretty lewd close up. 'I'll be back, laddie,' he confided at the top of his voice, waving his empty syringe like a broadsword. 'I favour the left buttock,' he concluded. 'Also known as the back-entry manoeuvre.'

With that, he charged off in search of a refill and left me to my own devices.

I made my way to the first floor. Hardy-Laing-free, it was a comparative haven of peace. I didn't have to look far, as Stern's door was thankfully open. A huge room, bare except for the desk

142

at which he sat, hunched over, manically tapping a keyboard. I coughed politely. No response. I went in and approached him tentatively, continuing to cough every few steps. Still no response, even when I stood right behind him. Awestruck, I glanced over his shoulder and read, 'A Man Walks Into a Horse: Comedy and Subversion'.

That's all I managed. Great title, though. Must be his new book. I was about to read on when I heard the stamp of approaching footsteps.

'I'm coming, laddie!' The voice got louder. 'My syringe is fully loaded.' The voice got louder still. 'No innuendo where none intended.'

Stern typed frantically on. I hurried over to the window and yanked it up just as Hardy Laing appeared in the doorway with a hefty male companion.

'Nurse Hector here will give you a quick swab,' he bellowed. 'Innuendo intended, I assure you!'

He tested his syringe with a quick squirt.

'Troosers doon the noo!'

Difficult to describe my feelings as I hit the gravel below. Relief, mainly, and a sprained ankle. I pedalled furiously off with the proprietor's final bellow reverberating in my ears.

'Do you question my methods?!'

I didn't, but I do. On the positive side, I'd managed to escape a full course of treatment. I began to shake violently as I escaped along Seafield Road, but relaxed as soon as I reached Vernon Avenue. I stopped the bike, safe at last, and went for a coffee at that nice little café on the corner. I had a great deal to mull over as I broke the top off a blueberry muffin. Comfort food? Possibly. I'd ordered six.

My main concern involved the allegedly learned Professor. He wasn't, it would appear, attached to an accredited university, yet he'd been my comedy guru for some time. I'd read all his papers. His *Learned Disquisition* was my bible. But what if, as seemed to be the case, he wasn't a real professor? Did this invalidate his theories? They're the same theories, you might argue, but without the rubber stamp of academic approval. Had I simply fled the hell of Hardy Laing – I haven't described Nurse Hector in all his nightmarish detail as I don't want the present publication to be filed under horror – for the mental hell of having my most cherished belief that the universe is essentially a comic construct, and that the possibly fraudulent Professor Emeritus Larry Stern is our earthly guide, demolished? A pretty unwieldy sentence, but it was a pretty unwieldy thought.

Then it struck me. A blinding flash of insight. I'd just reached the moist centre of my fifth muffin and swallowed it unchewed. The blinding flash? Great comedy ferments, not in the hallowed groves of academe, but the madhouse. This, for me, was a hugely cathartic moment. The Professor was back on top. I'd never doubt his learned word again.[18]

[18] See *The Annotated Sloot* for further reading. World as madhouse. Failed efforts of philosophy, religion, science to explain same. Suggestion that if we accept Hardy Laing's dictum that 'only the mad are truly insane', and further accept the three aunts' assertion that 'the whole world has gone skitherum ditherum, Hayding', then Stern's theories make perfect sense.

28

Back to three days later. Eddie's open-plan living room. Evening. Bottles of fizzy water sat on the kitchen worktop. The three aunts fussed around in their Bewley's uniforms. Quick twirl as they came in. 'Look, Hayding. No motballs.' Trace sat on Eddie's chair as if she owned it and cast what may have been lovelorn glances at Hayden. Or perhaps she was just making sure he steered clear of Eddie's Sweet Ambrosia. The aunts didn't seem to think so.

'Oh now.'

'Will you look at the two lovebirdies.'

'Tweet tweet, Hayding.'

A poignant little love scene, perhaps, but Hayden was too nervous to notice. What if no-one else turned up? He needed the killer there, whoever the killer was, and he needed him or, in the event of him being Marina, her, to crack. He had his modus operandi. All he needed now were the dramatis personae.

He did a bit of fussing around himself. Opened the cellar door, checked the light bulb worked, peered in. It looked suitably ghoulish when you knew what had taken place in its subterranean depths. Satisfied, he closed the door and turned his attention to the front window. Pascal O'Dea walked timidly up the drive. He hadn't been invited but maybe, just maybe, he might come in useful. He knocked apologetically. Hayden opened the door. Behind Pascal, compounding their possible guilt as a double act, came Lou Brannigan and Marina. Cop and escort? Pimp and whore? There was something about them; a certain intimacy that didn't quite add up, but Hayden didn't know what that intimacy was, and he didn't know what it didn't add up to.

They followed Pascal in and soon, thanks to a subdued Trace, everyone was drinking sparkling water and looking uneasy. Trace had removed the alcohol from the room, and Hayden hadn't supplied any food. Well, apart from the nuts. He'd supplied nuts. Some bash.

Lou Brannigan fingered his hat expectantly. Hayden had added a PS to Brannigan's invitation: '*Frankie Pope invited. Look forward to seeing you.*'

A knock on the door. Hayden went to answer. Enter Frankie.

'Sorry I'm late,' he said. 'Bit of business I had to attend to.'

Brannigan perked up. 'I'm sure there was,' he said. 'Isn't there always with you people? But how's this for a leading question? What, precisely, brings *you* here?'

A question to which Lou Brannigan already knew the answer. Typical cop. Frankie smiled enigmatically, which had the effect of making Hayden think, what if Brannigan was right? Frankie seemed to have forged a deep bond with Eddie. He didn't seem the type for murder. But what exactly *was* the type? What if Frankie was just a very clever, manipulative, unreconstructed Pope? Hayden looked around the room. The three aunts by the window, Trace in Eddie's chair, Frankie Pope now standing by the fireplace, Pascal smiling timidly near the worktop, Marina settled on the sofa and Lou Brannigan perched beside her on the arm.

Hayden clinked his glass with a spoon – a spoon he'd secreted in his pocket earlier for that precise purpose – and coughed.

'What brings *you* here? A good question, and one which applies to everyone in this room. Because I summoned you all, if that's the right word, under false pretences.'

Marina smiled mischievously. 'Oh goody,' she said. 'Would you like us to gasp?'

'That won't be necessary,' said Hayden.

Marina was being playful, but Hayden was on edge. This was serious stuff. A man had been murdered. The killer was in this very room. Stick to the set script.

He put his glass down, moved theatrically to stage centre, and waved the spoon for silence.

'A man has been murdered,' he declaimed. 'And the killer,' – he paused for dramatic effect – 'is in this very room.'

Lou Brannigan chortled genially and nodded at Hayden's hand. 'Would that be the murder weapon?' he said.

Hayden glowered at Dublin's finest, who was probably more used to these things than he was. He pocketed the spoon. Bit of an oversight. On the plus side, he still had the moral high ground. The three aunts came to his rescue.

'Oh, very good, Hayding.'

'In this very room.'

'Anyone fancy a nut?'

Despite all evidence to the contrary, Hayden was very fond of his aunts – but this was no time for nuts.

'In this very room,' he declaimed again. 'And no-one leaves till culpability is apportioned and the guilty party unmasked.'

'Janey! Is he wearing a mask, is he Hayding?'

Hayden withered them with a look. 'The mask is metaphorical, ladies. The 'he' assumptive. He could, after all, be a she. Or,' – and he made sure not to make eye contact with Frankie Pope – 'a bit of both. First question. What do we know about the murderer?' Hayden absently accepted a nut from the passing bowl – it discouraged further interruption – and fingered it meditatively as he spoke.

'Let's call him 'she'. Language fluidity. Why not?' He tossed the nut from one hand to the other as if to drive the point home. 'Which leaves us where? Driven by motive or motives unknown, our murderer, also known as 'she', enters the house with malice aforethought –'

'Malice aforetought. You've certinly got the gift, Hayding.'

'– while Eddie, hereinafter referred to as "the murderee". is otherwise engaged. Possibly painting in the shed. We may never know. The murderer also knows that Eddie is the only person likely to use the cellar. She opens the door –'

'– wit malice aforetought –'

'– like so.'

Hayden opened the door dramatically with his free hand. Vermilion light lit up the doorframe like vaporous blood. The colour of guilt. He looked quickly from face to face. They all seemed vaguely red and slightly squinty-eyed. No clue there. Frankie Pope strolled over and peered in.

'Impressive,' he said. 'Reminds me a bit of Tate Modern.'

The three aunts followed him over and gave it their earnest consideration.

'I tink we might lean more towards the more august Galleria Borghese and Caravaggio's middle period, Hayding.'

'Wonderful talent. Reputed to be gay.'

'But we might beg to differ.'

Hayden motioned Lou Brannigan and Marina over. Brannigan waved him away dismissively.

'We've seen enough,' he said.

Interesting, thought Hayden. They'd seen enough, yet they hadn't seen anything. Or had they? He felt he was on his way.

'Our perp, killer, call her what you will, proceeds to grab hold of the ladder and saw through the upright –'

'– wit a saw, Hayding.'

'A metal saw. Precisely.'

'Which she just happens to have secreted on her persing.'

'Possibly up her sleeve, Hayding, the way those old schoolmasters used to hide their canes up their jackets and you'd get a bit sticking up at the top, like a big pointy lump on their shoulder.'

'She found a saw in Eddie's toolbox.' Hayden glowered at his aunts. Silence. Back to Hayden. 'To recapitulate, she proceeds to saw through the upright, shrewdly leaving enough of it uncut to require more than one visit to the cellar to cause the final snap, thus facilitating a time gap between the act and its desired outcome. Clever. Fiendishly clever. Which brings us to our first suspect.' He scanned the room. Pascal. He'd start with Pascal. Keep it light. Introduce an element of comedy into the proceedings – he was a comedian, after all, it was what he did – and lull the killer into a false sense of security. 'Now what do we know about Pascal O'Dea?'

'She's a he, Hayding.'

'Difficult to know these days,' quipped Hayden. 'Dodgy ground. Pascal?' Pascal tittered shrilly. 'I'll take that as a he.' He gave Pascal a mock hard stare and absently fondled his nut. 'I suspected I'd found my man when Pascal visited me at Eddie's and said, "I killed your uncle". He then proceeded to divulge all the facts of the case. Insider knowledge. Eddie out. Cellar steps. Saw. Not to mention the masterfully devious delaying tactic. Question: how could he possibly know all this if he wasn't there? He must have done it. He even signed a detailed confession to that effect. Case closed –'

'Oh, well done, Hayding.'

'– you might be forgiven for thinking. Then I remembered. I'd met Bram at the Nautical Buoy. Bram. Old friend. Couldn't be here. Late shift. Anyway, I laid out all the facts before Bram at a table by the window. Confidentially.' He peered at Pascal over Áine Ní Cheannáin's imaginary half-glasses. 'For his ears only. However, and it's a big however, in the middle of our deliberations a man asked if we were using the salt. High-pitched voice. Nervous titter.' Pascal tittered nervously. 'We weren't using the salt. I told him so. I waved it away and returned to laying out the facts. Hush-hushly.' Hayden removed the imaginary half-glasses, mentally, for dramatic effect. 'But the man didn't take it. How do I know this? I've replayed the scene several times in my head. The salt stayed where it was. *Every time.*' He jabbed an accusing finger at Pascal. 'I put it to you that it was *you* who asked for the salt. *You* who didn't take it. That you subsequently confessed to the murders of Martin Luther King, Julius Caesar and your own father with the belt of a loy. That you couldn't possibly have been in Memphis or Ancient Rome in 1968 and 44BC respectively; that the father you confessed to murdering was, in fact, a fictional character from *The Playboy of the Western World*, a highly overrated play by JM Synge which has given we Irish a worldwide reputation for loquacious blather ever since. That you are a congenital liar and that, as a consequence, you are innocent of any and all charges relating to the murder of Edward McGlynn and are, as a further consequence, free to leave this room without a stain on your character.'

Hayden had got quite a head of steam up. He paused, then placed a hand gently on Pascal's shoulder. 'You may wish to change the air on Eddie's bicycle on your way out. Good for the inner tube.'

Pascal tittered happily as Hayden guided him towards the door and closed it behind him. Hayden then resumed his position at the centre of proceedings and carried on.

'Next, we come to my immediate family,' he said. 'My parents have lived in Waikiki for many years. They couldn't possibly have done it.' A hint of suppressed bitterness entered his voice. 'I haven't seen them since the day before my seventh birthday.'

'We remember it well, Hayding.'

'Bad blood.'

'But you're right.'

'They'd of needed a very long saw.'

'Not "they'd of", Dottie.'

'Florrie.'

'Don't change the subject. "They'd of" is totally meaningless.'

Florrie pouted, her little head shaking with indignation.

'Well, the existentialists would have us believe that *life* is totally meaningless, so what of it?'

'The existentialists were *French*, for pity's sake.'

'I suppose so.'

'And besides, I very much doubt if Ludwig Wittgenstein, whose specialty –'

'Speciality, but do go on.'

'– was language itself, would have countenanced the use of "they'd of" if he was standing in the room here today.'

'Which he isn't, being as what he's dead.'

'Dead he may be, Dodie, but –'

'I'm sure he was a wonderful lover, ladies,' said Hayden, 'but could we perhaps press on?'

29

The three aunts calmed down. A subdued Trace topped up the drinks. Hayden resumed.

'We next come to Frankie, aka Francis, Pope.'

Lou Brannigan chuckled silently. This he had to hear. Frankie remained impassive. He was giving nothing away.

'Frankie had a clear motive,' said Hayden. 'Revenge for humiliation.' Hayden avoided eye contact with Frankie and gave this time to sink in. 'Allow me.' He opened the back door and led them out into the garden. The late evening sun, almost autumnal in its melancholy russet hues, shone across Eddie's sculpted masterpiece, which now resembled nothing more or less than celebrated comic novelists Somerville and Ross. Time: 20.59. Against the back wall, Hayden had lined up several kitchen chairs in preparation. 'Now, if everyone would kindly hoick themselves up onto a chair, I'll explain exactly what I mean.'

They made their way to the bottom of the garden, past the statue, and did as bidden. Hayden avoided eye contact with Frankie. Guilty or innocent? He really wasn't sure any more. He stood on the chair in the centre and pointed at Frankie's living room.

'Observe,' he said.

The three aunts giggled in unison.

'We can't observe, Hayding.'

'Unless you want us to observe the wall.'

'Only we can't see over. It's a height ting.'[19]

---

[19] I've edited a bit here. 'Height is a feminist issue, Hayding. Discuss.' They did.

'So just describe the object of your observations wit your usual verbal eloquence.'

'Not to mention your natural talent for the felicitous turn of phrase.'

Hayden looked at them to see if they were being humorous. Difficult to tell. They stared blankly at the wall.

The learned Professor Stern devotes a whole chapter in his equally learned *Disquisition* to the deadpan school of comedy[20], including snapshot profiles of several leading practitioners of this most subtle of art forms. No mention of the aunts. Hayden kept an open mind and wound back.

'Observe,' he repeated. 'Frankie Pope's living room. Observe the painting above the mantelpiece.'

'No, Hayding. We don't. But do carry on.'

Lou Brannigan coughed politely. 'Neither do we.'

Hayden looked closer. Good point. The painting was gone.

Frankie Pope shifted uneasily. 'That bit of business I was referring to earlier. I was putting it back in the shed.'

'I see.' It was now Hayden's turn to look sheepish. 'Follow me,' he said. 'No chairs required.'

He led them to the shed. It was beginning to look like a conducted tour of the Great Man's estate, which, in a funny sort of way, it was. He opened the shed door and ushered them inside. Frankie had placed Eddie's portrait on an easel in pride of place.

'Oh, very dramatic, Hayding.'

'The setting, the wooden surrounds, the serendipitous presence of that golden orb, the sun.'

'All conspiring to suffuse Eddie's final artwork wit a look of permanence, of history yet modernity.'

'Of den-ness, if you will, yet now-ness.'

'As if it had just been painted yet, simultaneously, always existed.'

---

[20] Prof. Larry Stern, *Disquisition*, Chapter LXXI – *The Mask That Freezes the Face*.

Beautifully put. The aunts certainly knew their art but, as with nuts, now was not the time. Hayden coughed for silence.

'*Portrait of a Lady*,'[21] he began. 'Magnificent living room. Marble mantelpiece. Now, train your eyes on the sitter or, more accurately, stander. An elegant woman in Victorian attire. Hair just so. Subtly lit in muted hues suggesting a bygone age. At her feet, beside the fireplace, a sleeping dog. A nineteenth century masterpiece acquired by the Pope family at Christie's of London for an undisclosed sum, perhaps? Not so. The painting was recently purloined by, or, put it another way –'

He looked straight at Frankie Pope. Frankie Pope looked straight back.

'Nicked,' Frankie said. 'I know what purloined means.' Hayden made eye contact with Lou Brannigan, for the record. But Frankie hadn't finished. 'Eddie bequested it to me verbally. Then he died, so I, well, I...' Frankie paused to repress what might have been a sob. 'But it's been eating away at me. Theft, you know? It's not my way. Never has been.' Brannigan snorted. Frankie ignored him and carried on. 'So I had a quick think. What would Eddie say? "I died at a bad time for you, Frankie. Take it on the chin, lad. Put it back."'

Frankie left it there. Hayden pressed on.

'To continue,' he said, 'look closer at the painting. The dog in question is Rusty.' Rusty barked as if to confirm this. 'Good dog. My point? This is no nineteenth century masterpiece but an authentic Eddie McGlynn. The portrait in question is not some titled lady from a bygone age. Why, the lady in question is none other than – look closer – Frankie Pope her – sorry, *him*self.'

'Sure we know that, Hayding.'

'We were there when he stood for the sitting.'

Hayden ignored the three aunts. He was in full flow. 'Here's a plausible theory,' he said. 'Eddie painted a member of the notorious Pope fraternity as a woman. Bit of a laugh for Frankie,

[21] Subtitle: *A Man's a Man for a' That.*

perhaps. Bit of a wheeze.' Frankie looked upset, but Hayden was now committed. Best to carry on. 'Frankie, however, lived to regret it. Eddie had undermined his masculinity. This, in the cold light of sobriety, was an act of deep and ritual humiliation for a man in his position. In an effort to make sure this folly on his part went no further, Frankie nicked the painting.'

'Purloined,' said Frankie. 'We've been through all that.'

'But that wasn't all,' said Hayden. 'No. Instead of destroying the evidence, he put the painting on his mantelpiece, possibly for one last loving look. Great painting, and it was, after all, him. Bad move; the reaction of his siblings, who may have popped round for a surprise visit, was apoplexy all round. Inference? In World of Mafioso or Irish equivalent, he had to do away with Eddie to reclaim his manhood.'

Lou Brannigan gave Hayden an approving look. 'Good man yourself,' he said. 'Full marks. I'll just contact the lads if, that is,' – he turned to Frankie – 'it's all the same with yourself.'

Frankie looked sadly at Hayden. Hayden looked away. He'd started down a particular route, so he might as well see where it led.

'However,' he continued, 'if Frankie Pope had wanted to do away with Eddie, why didn't he just blast him with an Uzi?'

Marina tutted playfully. 'Perish the thought. It's not that sort of area.'

Well you can talk, *Madam*. Hayden almost said this, but Brannigan was giving him the hard cop stare. 'Let's get this straight,' he said. 'Are you suggesting our friend here didn't do it?'

Hayden held the shed door open and ushered everyone out. The sun was sinking low in a magnificent fiery blaze over the garden, and Eddie's masterpiece now resembled legendary folkloric heroine Queen Méabh in full battle dress. Not that anyone noticed. They were too busy waiting for Hayden's reply. He closed and bolted the door, then walked slowly towards the house, savouring the tension afforded by stretching the term 'dramatic pause' to the outer limits of its meaning. They re-entered the house. Trace reached for the sparkling water, but Hayden coughed politely and she backed off. Hayden stood in the centre of the room and waited until they were all settled in place, Frankie sitting on the sofa this time as if upset by the whole business.

Hayden then resumed. 'Frankie loved Eddie,' he said. 'Eddie was his mentor. He loves the painting. It takes a bit of getting used to, but Frankie is in touch with his feminine side. So no, he didn't kill Eddie.'

A rejuvenated Frankie clapped his hands on his knees and stood up. 'Glad that's sorted,' he said, heading to the door. 'Anyway, got to go. Bit of business to attend to.'

Lou Brannigan chuckled knowingly. 'I'll bet you do,' he said. 'I'll bet you do.'

Frankie gave him the soft stare. 'Advanced art class at nine,' he said. 'I promised Eddie.' He pointed a playful finger at Brannigan and cocked his thumb. Not so much 'gotcha' as 'touché'. Then he was gone. Brannigan looked puzzled. He turned his attention to Hayden.

'Hold on there a miniscule minyute,' he said. 'You've called us here to unmask an alleged killer. Someone in this very room, quote unquote. So if mister-our-friend there didn't do it, then who in the name of Saint Mother Teresa *did* in your expert and, I'd have to say, gasbag-of-the-feckin-year opinion?'

Hayden overlooked the fact that the 'Mother' bit had been dropped when the 'Saint' bit was added. This was no time for verbal niceties. He jabbed an accusatory finger at Detective Inspector Lou Brannigan.

'You did.'

30

Dramatic stuff, which is why I added a chapter break. The action is continuous, but Hayden's bombshell is a lot to take in.

'I *did*?' said Brannigan. '*I* did? Are you demented entirely? That's some accusation, mister. I'll tell you something, and you can keep it to yourself or spread it round the world on social meejah if the fancy takes you, but next time I pour a pot of tea on your testicularities –'

The three aunts giggled as one woman.

'So *that* explains the stain, Hayding. Only we were wondering.'

'You know. Man of a certing age.'

'Well that's a blessèd relief anyway. You had us worried there on the continence front.'

'Sorry, Constable. You were saying?'

'Detective Inspector if it's all the same to you. The term Constable left this particular megalopolis with the last vestiges of perfidious Albion.' Brannigan's mobile went. He answered it. 'What? Well whaddya know. That'll be the curse o' God Popes. I'll be straight over.' He shoved his mobile into his pocket and relaxed back into himself. 'Incident in darkest Coolock,' he said. 'I suppose I'd better show willing.'

He started at a leisurely pace for the door, but the three aunts weren't having it.

'Ah now, fair's fair, Deputy.'

'You've just been accused of murder.'

'Exonerate yourself, or fess up and turn yourself in to the relevant autorities.'

'To wit, yourself.'

They started giggling like peewits on helium. Lou Brannigan ignored them and turned to Hayden. 'You have two minyutes. And it had better be good, because I'll tell you for why. I've never killed Eddie McGlynn in my life.'

Hayden looked around. He was running out of suspects. It had to be Brannigan. Or Brannigan and Marina. Or Marina. Their story just didn't make sense otherwise. He drew on all his skills as a performer, polished the nut absently on his jacket, and outlined his cast iron case. 'It all started,' he began, 'with this.'

He walked over to the answering machine and pressed play. They waited. A husky female voice: 'You haven't settled up yet, Eddie. So call Marina. I really must insist.' A short pause. The voice dropped a register. 'Or else, my sweet. Or else.'

Hayden studied Brannigan and Marina closely while the message played.

'This message was left several weeks ago, *before* the fatal incident. What was I to make of that? I wasn't sure. Who was this Marina? What did she mean by settle up?' He dropped his voice to a gravelly whisper. '"Or else, my sweet. Or else."'

'Questions questions questions, Hayding. And you wanted answers.'

'Was it den you decided to become a sloot, was it Hayding?'

'Sorry, Hayding. More questions.'

'Good news about the trousers, dough. You had us worried there.'

'But do carry on.'

Hayden carried on. 'I checked with my old and trusted friend Bram. Did he know a Marina?'

'Oh now, Hayding. Say no more.'

'By which we mean pray continue.'

Hayden continued. 'Bram, to my surprise, came over all coy.' He looked accusingly at Marina. 'And no wonder.'

'He doesn't look the type, Hayding. But I suppose it takes all sorts. On you go.'

'"She lives across the road from Eddie's," said Bram. "The house with the rhododendrons. Big sign outside. Red coupé if the lady in question is in." I strolled up from the Nautical Buoy and Marina arrived bang on cue. Introductions over, she ordered me upstairs for a quote *double session*' – Trace gripped her bottle like a comfort blanket and blanched. She looked like someone who could use a stiff drink. Another couple of digits off her Twelve Point Plan? Hayden looked straight at Marina – 'unquote.'

'Did she indeed, Hayding?

'Oh now. And what do you suppose she meant by *that*?'

'I think we all know what she meant,' said Hayden. 'Marina, and I'm sure she'll back me up on this, is a whore.'

'Janey times tree, Hayding. We speak as one.'

'A whore?' said Brannigan menacingly. 'Is that a factual fact?'

Marina smiled at Hayden. An enigmatic smile. 'Do go on,' she said. 'You build a compelling case.'

'Anyway, there I stood, stunned,' continued Hayden. 'Enter Detective Inspector Lou Brannigan. Cue an *outrageously* implausible red herring about missing cats.'

'Cats and fish in the same sentence, Hayden,' smiled Marina. 'I'm impressed.'

Hayden experienced an unbidden frisson at her use of his name. He sublimated and ploughed on. 'DI Brannigan, to continue, also ordered me to do what the lady said.'

'Go upstairs, you naughty Hayding.'

'Divest yourself of your outer cloding fortwit.'

She didn't say anything of the sort, but Hayden let the three aunts have their little moment. Which, as with everything else to do with the aunts, he would shortly live to regret.

'It might have all been perfectly innocent, Hayding. The lovely lady might have wanted him to wash your trousers for you.'

'As he was responsible for the stain in the first place.'

Hayden gave his aunts a cold look. 'Point of information. The pot-of-tea-on-trousers scene came later. At this stage in the proceedings, there was no stain. Brannigan was covering for the "lovely lady", for reason or reasons unknown.' He glowered at Brannigan, then addressed a final summing up to the room. 'Reason or reasons unknown.' He paused to let the repetition sink in. 'Or were they? I put it to you that the aforementioned Marina is a whore, that this alleged upholder of the law of the land is her pimp, that the answerphone message was a thinly-veiled threat, the result of which,' – he lifted the empty urn from the table – 'you see before you. I rest my case.'

Trace glanced over at Marina. She seemed, from her expression, to delight in Marina's guilt. The three aunts, enraptured by Hayden's rhetoric, were about to lead the applause, but Brannigan got in there first.

'Persuasively argued,' he said. He put a protective arm around Marina and spoke to her with uncharacteristic gentleness. 'Will you demolish it, kiddo, or will I?' Rhetorical question. Detective Inspector Lou Brannigan had the floor and he intended to keep it that way.

'To understand the little scene outlined by our intrepid sleuth here,' he began, 'which, by the way, is incorrect in every particular, we need to take a trip back into the past. To the precise moment I found out I was adopted.' Marina sighed but said nothing. 'To that moment when I discovered a letter from my,' – Brannigan choked with emotion – 'a letter from my,' – Marina squeezed his hand – 'my mother, in the adoption papers. A letter I have since kept close to my tear-stained heart.'

Tear-stained heart? Steady on there. Nobody said this, of course. The moment was too raw. Too emotionally charged.

Lou Brannigan rooted in his breast pocket and took out his wallet. From the wallet he removed a folded piece of plastic and from the plastic he produced a faded sheet. He opened it out and held it with trembling hands.

'"Dear Son,"' he read, '"I've been a sinful woman, so I'm away off to England. When you get this letter in years to come, and I know you will, Son, I want you to find your little sister and look after her."' He glanced over at Marina with genuine adoration. '"She was born six minutes after you. Love, Mammy."' His eyes, which had long since shed any remaining seen-it-all cynicism, welled up. '"PS. I call you 'son', Son, because I'll never know you or your sister's names."'

Trace turned away and sobbed into her sleeve. The three aunts looked distraught.

'We're twins too, Chief Inspector.'

'I'm ninety-six, Dodie is ninety-four, and Dottie here is ninety-two.'

'Florrie. You're Dottie. The ting is dough, we feel your pain.'

'I appreciate that,' said Brannigan, wiping away what he saw as an unmanly tear. 'We stayed together till we were three weeks old. Totally inseparable. Then my little sister was adopted by the Courtneys of Westmeath.'

Hayden started. 'The Courtneys?'

'That's what I said,' continued Brannigan. 'The stud farm folk. I, on the other hand, was raised by a family in West Cork. The Brannigans. Decent, God-fearing souls, but I always felt somehow different. As if I was missing an arm or something. Cut to the discovery' – Lou Brannigan almost broke down here. This big, lumbering, wounded orphan who had worked his way to the top of his profession was now almost weeping openly

'the discovery of Mammy's letter. I got straight onto *Twins Reunited.*' He drew Marina close. Proudly. Protectively. 'The result,' he said, 'you see before you here tonight. The missing arm turned out to be this... this adorable...'

The room was awash with empathy. The aunts applauded. Trace, overcome with the tragedy of it all, blew her nose. But Hayden was agitated.

'This is all very well,' he declaimed loudly, bringing all eyes back to him, 'but it doesn't explain' – he pointed an accusing finger at the telephone – 'this.'

'No, Hayden,' said Marina, 'but perhaps *this* does.'

She crossed the room to where a stack of Eddie's paintings leaned against the wall and motioned to a speedily recovering Brannigan.

'Would you?'

Brannigan wiped his eyes with a jacket sleeve and beamed at her. He riffled through the stack, removed an unframed painting, and held it aloft with his huge Garda hands. It depicted Mary Magdalene draped seductively across a divan with Christ, one hand on a motel doorknob, the other held up in a gesture of denial: '*I Must Be About My Father's Business*,' read Marina. '*Eddie McGlynn. Oil on Canvas.*'

Hayden was floored.

'I was very fond of Eddie,' said Marina, 'but he never looked after himself. Sometimes he went days without eating. So I agreed to sit for him on one condition: payment was dinner at my restaurant of choice. I was looking forward to it, so I left a message. It was meant to be playful, Hayden. Mischievous.' She sighed at the memory. 'Eddie, you see, was such a wonderful – oh, what's the term?'

Hayden tried the bullish approach. 'Client?'

'Life force,' said Marina. 'Sadly, he never got the message.'

'So perhaps,' said Brannigan, 'you'd like to reconsider your original verdict. I seem to recall the word 'pimp' being bandied about.'

Marina placed her hand on Brannigan's arm. A soothing gesture. She turned to Hayden. 'I'm a Jungian psychoanalyst, Hayden. Specialising in the mother complex.' She gazed fondly up at Brannigan. 'You see, Lou –'

Brannigan gave her a pained look. 'Please.'

Marina smiled professionally and said nothing. The confidentiality of the couch.

Hayden was stunned. 'Hold on,' he said. 'This doesn't make sense. Tell you what. Take five. Back in a tick.'

He went to the front door, swung it open, and marched briskly down the drive. He crossed the road, walked up to Marina's gate and yanked the rhododendron bush away from the sign.

Marina : Courtney

He didn't bother reading on. Courtesan. Courtney. Bloody rhododendrons. And the colon? Not a colon at all, but a couple of rusty screws fastening the board to a stake. But hold on. His mind was in overdrive. This wasn't over yet. He strode back to Eddie's, went in and closed the front door dramatically. He repositioned himself in the centre of the room.

'Okay,' he said. 'Okay. You're a psychoanalyst, so what was all that about the oldest profession on the phone? You can hardly deny it.' The three aunts were about to burst into a fresh fit of giggles, but Hayden wasn't having it. 'I think you'll find, ladies, that the oldest profession is prostitution. First recorded over four thousand years ago, apparently. I'm surprised you didn't know that.' You were probably there at the time. He didn't say the last bit, but he kept it in reserve.

'Not so, Hayding. We mean, work it out for yourself.'

'There's Adam, crunching into a Granny Smit, when he tinks, hold on, tings are getting a bit predictable around here. I wonder should I visit a whore?'

'Then he tinks, no, I'm a one-woman man.'

'Which is just as well when you tink about it.'

'As our American cousins say, Hayding, do the mat.'

'But that leads him to a further tought.'

'I wonder who the mammy was?'

'He tinks, Janey, the only woman in the whole world is my own lovely wife Eve. Am I after knowing my own mammy?'

'In the biblical sense, Hayding.'

'Put it another way. Am I after propagating the species incestually?'

'He tries to sublimate this tought. No use. His oul sex drive is shot. He takes to the bottle.'

'Only it's not a bottle in those days, Hayding. Let's call it a gourd.'

'Well whatever it is, Hayding, it's a cry for help.'

'He works it trew.'

'Eureka moment.'

'"I'm after sleeping wit my own beloved mammy! Anyone know a good psychoanalyst?"'

'Enter Eve. "Lie back on that grass hillock there, Adam. Now, what seems to be the problem?"'

'And there you have it. Psychoanalysis, the oldest profession.'

'Invented, mark you, by a female lady.'

'One-nil to the early feminist movement.'

'We rest our case.'

They may have stopped there, but it didn't matter. Hayden wasn't listening. He was studying the floorboards, totally deflated. He'd made a complete idiot of himself *and* he was nowhere nearer locating the killer.

Not Pascal.

Not Frankie Pope.

Not Brannigan and Marina.

Who next? Trace? Trace was a stalker and patently unstable, but did that make her a killer? She was clearly obsessed with Hayden, her alcohol fixation a possible manifestation of her warped desire to control him – which might just involve the ultimate control: murder. But Eddie? She'd never even met Eddie. Besides, she was probably in London at the time of his death. Bit of a long shot.

Which left the three aunts, and there was no way they could have done it.

Or was there?

Hayden sized them up. Tiny. Well into their nineties. Possibly older. Didn't women always lie about their age? He replayed in his mind their various meetings over the past few days. The slinking, the scurrying, the scuttling. The furtive glances and shifty eyes. All signs of possible guilt. And then it came back to him. The tiny feet at dawn. The missing tape. Hardly proof of fratricide; on the other hand it must have been them, mainly because it wasn't anyone else. Hayden decided to tackle them head on. Apart from anything, it would put him back in control of proceedings – or so he thought. This was one valuable lesson he learned from the whole sorry business: in dealing with his three dearly beloved but inscrutable aunts, it doesn't pay to think.

'We finally come,' he said, 'to my three venerated, not to say sainted, aunts. Step forward, ladies. Now. I first had my suspicions when you started behaving strangely about me staying at Eddie's. You were desperate to stop me staying overnight. Why?'

'Well, Hayding –'

'The question is rhetorical. I'll answer it myself in due course. You also seemed perturbed when I claimed to have solved the case, only to brighten visibly when it became apparent that I hadn't. Why? And then I hear intruders at five o'clock in the morning, rooting surreptitiously, as I now have reason to believe, through Eddie's tapes. Why? I put it to you that the answer to all three questions is one and the same. You have something to hide. And this brings us back to that bizarre incident at the funeral. You deleted the photo of Eddie. Why? I put it to you that you wanted to maintain the fiction that Eddie died of natural causes. Why?' He grabbed a lapel with his nut-free hand and paused to let the question resonate. 'Because, I put it to you one last and final time, you killed him!'

The three aunts were mightily impressed.

'Oh, very good, Hayding.'

'Hayding McGlynn, King of the Sloots.'

'Il sloot di tooty sloot.'

'And not unreminiscent of the Ancient Greek orator Cicero in his finest hour.'

Florrie blushed.

'I take it you're referring to the time we –'

'No, Dottie. I'm not. I'm referring to his finest *oratorical* hour. *Pro Archia Poeta*.'

Florrie bridled.

'No oratoricals when *I* was around, I can assure you.'

A momentary pause while they composed themselves. Spat over, they turned their attention back to Hayden.

'But what's our motivation?'

'Maybe we just didn't like the cut of Eddie's jib.'

'What's a jib?'

'I tink it's in the Bible. If the cut of thy jib offend thee, pluck it out.'

'That's thy right eyeball, silly. If thy right –'

'Silence!' barked Hayden. He felt he was losing control, possibly because he was, and Brannigan was the first to break ranks.

'Get a grip of yourself, man,' he said, walking to the door. 'I've known these ladies since they were in their late sixties and I'll tell you one thing. There's not a blemish on their characters. Good, upstanding, God-fearing spinsters of this parish. Mass every morning. Confession twice daily. You ought to be ashamed of yourself.'

And with a last look to check that Hayden was, indeed, ashamed of himself, he was gone.

Marina hesitated before leaving too. She slipped over to Hayden and put a hand on his arm. A subtle erotic charge, intentional or not, passed from hand to arm. 'Erwin Schrödinger,' she smiled. 'Who'd have thought?' She squeezed him gently. 'Anything I can do for you in return,' she continued. 'Any time.' She smiled her enigmatic smile. 'Double session. No need to book.'

With that she freed his arm, unplugging, if you will, the erotic charge, and she too was gone. Hayden sighed an involuntary, lovelorn sigh and so, in perfect synchronicity, did Trace; the sigh, in her case, concealing a wild, internal, cry of pain. She screwed the top off a bottle of sparkling water, poured it tremblingly, tearfully, down the sink, and followed the others out.

31

Hayden stood alone in the sitting room. Well, apart from the three aunts, who looked out the front window and giggled with girlish glee.

'Mass every morning, Hayding? We tink not.'

'And all that guff about blemishes. Sure we're covered in blemishes, Hayding.'

'We were up for gun running in the tirties.'[22]

'To be fair, that was before his time, but he's way off beam on the character front.'

'We mean to say, what sort of training do they give police bobbies these days at all?'

'It's no wonder the country is —'

'Language, Dottie. He's at an impressionable age.'

But Hayden wasn't listening. Again. He was routed, his humiliation complete.

'Ah, will you look at the little face on him. Poor Hayding.'

'I suppose he'll want to know what really happened now.'

'Mind you, *we* don't know.'

'On account of the dementia.'

Their little heads bobbed mischievously.

'Or do we?'

Hayden closed his eyes, shook his head wearily, and finally swallowed the nut. It was the last thing he'd eat for several days.

Seconds later, Hayden opened his eyes. The three aunts stood in a row facing him, their six tiny eyes trained on his.

---

[22] Spanish Civil War, to clarify.

'This is pretty heavy duty stuff, Hayding.'

'Maybe you'd like to sit down.'

Hayden bridled. 'I'll stand, if it's all the same with you. I can take it.'

'That's all very well, Hayding. But can *we*?'

'We've been getting cricks in our necks ever since you started your pontifications.'

'You must be what? At least five tree.'

'Five feet nine and a half,' said Hayden. The if-you-don't-mind was implied in his tone. He sat down.

'Good boy.'

'You always were a good boy under all that braggadocio.'

'And the holier-than-thou stuff in your twenties when dialectical materialism was de rigueur wit the pseudo-intellectuals. Not to mention – but that can wait for happier times.'

'Here's the nub of the ting, Hayding. We *were* up to no good.'

'We can't remember any of it on account of the dementia, but sometimes we get little flashes.'

'Hold on, girls, I tink I'm getting one now.'

'Me too. Don't say me tree, Florrie, or I'll burst you.'

'Dottie, if you don't mind. We knew you were going trew the tapes, Hayding, so we popped in when we tought you'd be asleep and took the incrimulating one.'

Hayden was on his feet again. 'The incrimulating one? You mean –'

'We do mean, Hayding. The one that incrimulates.'

Dottie – could have been Dodie – took a reel-to-reel tape from her handbag and slotted it back on the tape shelf.

'However, we took the liberty of transferring it to the latest gadgetry.'

'Modering technology, Hayding. Little hobby of ours.'

They produced a small state of the art doodah. I'm not up on these things myself, but when they switched it on! The *sound*! Mono recording, Sensurround effect. You know, that thing you get in the cinema when you'd swear the baddie was behind you.

Hayden sat down again and swallowed hard. Were the three aunts about to confess to murder, that most heinous of crimes? What would he do if they did? Shop them? The other inmates wouldn't last five minutes if they were banged up with this lot.

They set the small gadget down on the table and beamed reassuringly at Hayden. He didn't beam back.

'This is the edited version, Hayding. Location: Eddie McGlynn's domicile.'

'We cut the toilet breaks.'

They pressed play. Two voices. Both incredibly drunk. Hayden recognised them immediately.

EDDIE: Go aisy on the drink there, son. It's not a competition. Where was I? Ah yes. I followed your career with interest. Hoping. Always hoping.

HAYDEN: Sorry, but what the fuck do you mean by that?

EDDIE: *Only Quotin'*? Big mistake. *Father Brown's Boys*? I know they killed you off, son, but have you ever watched it? And how about that leprechaun suit ad?

Hayden was stunned. Eddie was dredging up his long-buried past, but Hayden had no recollection whatsoever of this conversation, or when it had taken place. He listened on with dread.

HAYDEN: But – but that was, like, the start of my career. That was early fucking on.

It was too. He was the same age as Foetus O'Flaherty is now. On the make. Not thinking of the years of self-torture ahead.

EDDIE: Excuses, son. Excuses. The point at issue here is, the true artist doesn't compromise. I didn't bring you into the world to peddle pap to the masses.

SOUND OF A CHAIR HITTING THE FLOOR.

'I tink that was you falling over, Hayding.'

'We'll tell you one ting.'

'You're better at sitting down now.'

'Deliberately tirsty, Hayding. That's what you were in those days.'

'But – but I don't remember any of this.'

'Oh now, Hayding. Last time you were over. Six munts ago.'

Hayden was incensed. 'Wait a minute. I wasn't over six months ago.'

'You most certingly were, Hayding. You possibly don't remember, being as how you were hitting Eddie's Sweet Amnesia wit vim and gusto.'

'But back to the incrimulating tape.'

SOUND OF LIQUID BEING POURED.

HAYDEN: What do you mean 'bring me into the world'? You're a midwife all of a sudden?

'Pause here, Hayding.'

'Pretty pregnant to our way of tinking.'

'No pun intended, but stick around. It gets worse.'

EDDIE: You're right, son. I spoke out of turn.

HAYDEN: Son? Jesus! What's all this 'son' shit? What exactly the fuck are you on?

'Tut tut, Hayding. Tree genteel ladies present.'

'Although to be fair about it, we weren't present at the time.'

HAYDEN: What right have you to demolish my – to demolish my career you –

Hayden listened in pained silence as his past self stuttered to a furious, intoxicated, word-search stop.

HAYDEN: – you –

He was off again.

HAYDEN: – cunt.

The three aunts pressed pause.
'Lucky for you, he didn't play the tape back before he died,
Hayding. It would have killed the poor man.'
'We tought of cutting that bit.'
'But decided that, on balance, it added nuance.'
'Lovely word, nuance. Delicate. Playful.'
'Unlike 'cunt'. Which suggests to us, Hayding –'
'– you're better off the jungle juice.'
'Because on it, to be quite honest, you were always a bit of a –'
'Stop it, Dorrie.'
'Flottie. A bit of a –'
They composed themselves. Then pressed play.

EDDIE: Now stop it right there, son. You've no right to talk
to your fa –

'Second pregnant pause, Hayding.'

HAYDEN: My fa? What the fuck is a fa? You're not my
fucking –

'Pause numero tree, Hayding.'
'Wait for it. Any second now.'

HAYDEN: Da?

'End of act one, Hayding.'
'Beautiful twist, by the way.'
'But where can it go from here?'

32

I must say, I hadn't expected this. Was *Sloot*, I found myself wondering, a modern Irish tragedy? Hayden's life had certainly entered the realm of the Ancient Greeks. Granted, he wasn't high born in the Aristotelean sense if we're going to stick to rigid definitions. Perhaps, rather, he bears out Stern's most oft-quoted dictum: 'For what is comedy but tragedy with loose trousers?'

The sound of loud snores vibrated from the tape.

'Well there's your answer, Hayding. That's Eddie's considered response to the daddy question.'

'Inscrutable or what?'

'Oh yes. Very Zen.'

Hayden's animated voice cut across the snores.

HAYDEN: Jesus, that's it, isn't it? You *are* my fucking father. My dear old fucking da.

'And so it came to pass, Hayding.'

'Troot will out.'

'He *was* your dear old naughty word da.'

Hayden paced the floor, stunned into silence. He also paced the floor on tape. But ranting.

HAYDEN: I'll tell you what I'm going to do, you fucking old fucking fuck. I'm going to burn this place down with all your so-called masterpieces. That'll fucking larn you.

'The merest smidgeonette of professional jealousy there, poot-être?'

'It's nutting to be ashamed of, Hayding.'

'Perfectly acceptable in the arts world. Not to say de rigueur.'

'You were impugned.'

'Impugned, Hayding. His only begotting son. Him wit his genius and you wit your leprechaun suit.'

Hayden sank into the sofa as they leaned over the gadget and pressed tiny buttons with their equally tiny fingers.

'We cut a bit here. Opening drawers. Riffling, riffling, riffling.'

'Wit accompanying voiceover rant. A veritable tesaurus of naughty words.'

'Next bit. Are you sitting comfortably? Then we'll begin.'

HAYDEN: Are there no fucking matches in this house? I mean, Jesus! Does no-one fucking smoke anymore?

SOUND OF DRAWER BEING PULLED OUT AND SEVERAL OBJECTS SPILLING TO THE FLOOR. A DERANGED CACKLE.

HAYDEN: Is this a hacksaw I see before me, the handle towards my hand?

SOUND OF CELLAR DOOR CREAKING OPEN. FRANTIC SAWING AND MANIC GRUNTS.

HAYDEN: *Artist Descending into Hades*? He'll descend into Hades all right. His son and heir will see to that.

SAWING CONTINUES. GRAVELLY SNORES IN THE BACKGROUND. ANGRY SOBS. THE FRONT DOORBELL TINKLES. SAWING CONTINUES. DOORBELL TINKLES AGAIN. HAYDEN GROANS DRUNKENLY. SAWING STOPS. DRUNKEN FOOTSTEPS. DOOR OPENS.

BRAM: (MUFFLED) Late shift. Thought I'd drop by, see how you – bloody hell, had a few scoops, have we?

VOICES MOVE CLOSER.

HAYDEN: Juss a couple. Pour yourshelf a drop there, with you in a tick. Bit of a job to do first.

SAWING CONTINUES.

BRAM: You seem a bit upset.

SAWING INTENSIFIES.

BRAM: So, like, what exactly are you up to?

HAYDEN: What do you think I'm up to? Isn't it obvious what I'm fucking up to?

BRAM: Fair enough. Tell you what. Why don't you just leave it there for now, hoh? Take a break. Quick snooze maybe. You can always get back to it later.

'Oh, very emollient, Hayding. Good old Abraham.'

'He finally manages to settle you down. Cut to –'

A knock on the door. Hayden sat mesmerised. What now? What could possibly add to his misery? Another knock.

'That's not the tape knocker, Hayding. The tape is stopped. That's the *now* knocker.'

Hayden snapped out of his mesmeric state. 'Oh, right.'

He went to answer it. Bram. 'Late shift. Sorry I couldn't make it earlier. Good gig?' He followed Hayden into the living room. 'All over, is it?'

'Well! If it isn't little Abraham!'

'*You've* certingly shot up. And wearing long trousers to boot.'

'Quite the young gentleman about town.'

Bram heard this as white noise. Hayden was staring at him. Why? What had he done? He'd only just arrived. Hayden pointed an accusing finger at him.

'You knew all along. And you never said – you never said a word.'

Bram had his more-confused-than-usual face on. 'What?' he said. 'Knew what?'

'I sawed through the ladder. I. Killed. Eddie.'

'Oh, *that*,' said Bram. 'But sure you knew that. I mean, you were there at the time.'

Hayden stared at him, incredulous. 'I was *stocious*,' he all but wailed. 'Flootered. Steaming.'

The three aunts nodded their heads in unison.

'As drunk as a skunk in a bunk wit a monk, Abe.'

'But,' – Bram was totally stupefied – 'that's why I suggested the plot backwards device. You know who did it, so you work back.'

'That was the *novel*, Bram,' said Hayden, his voice plaintive. 'That,' he sighed, 'was *fiction*.'

'Was it? Oh. Right.' Bram scratched his wispy head. 'Was it?'

Hayden ignored him. He'd gone to a place beyond understanding. The three aunts put their mini sound system back in the handbag.

'So there y'are, Hayding. You managed to kill your very own daddy.'

They suddenly looked concerned.

'Ah, will you look at him, the poor boy.'

'You're like the Wreck of the Hesperus, Hayding.'

'Maybe we shouldn't have told him.'

'But don't worry, Hayding. There's no shame in it. Stalin twenty million, Hayding one.'

'See? You've got to put tings in perspective.'

'And while we're on the subject, Hayding, how's this for a double whammy?'

'Your mammy wasn't your mammy.'

'Gas, hoh?'

Hayden flumped onto the sofa. No. It wasn't gas. For him, at least, it was the opposite of gas. He put his metaphorical head in his metaphorical hands. In reality, he sat staring into nothingness. Catatonic.

'Ah, will you look at him. The poor boy.'

'It's a lot to take in, Hayding. But it's very simple at root.'

'Your mammy who isn't your mammy wanted a babby. Your daddy – ditto – wanted one too.'

'A small boy. Just like him.'

'Hayding Junior. It's a man ting.'

'So they done what you do.'

'Copulacious activities over a lengty period.'

'Nutting.'

'Tried everyting. *Kama Sutra.* Naughty fillums.'

'Still nutting.'

'Resorted to the inexplicable power of prayer.'

'"Oh Lord, we don't believe in a deity, benevolent, biblical or udder, but if you could see your way to giving us a babby or, if you will, to bringing fort issue in the case of McGlynn and McGlynn –"'

'"– we'd be happy to reconsider in the light of said munificence."'

'More nutting. So, in steps, Eddie. Unattached male. Blood relayshing. High sperm count.'

'Language *please.* There's a schoolboy present. Kindly remove your ears fortwit, Abraham –'

'– although on second toughts, he has to learn some time.'

'Very true. Ears as they were, Abe. Only don't say we told you. Anyway, Hayding, your daddy didn't want the fruit of your mammy's womb to come courtesy of his younger sibling brother doing the actual deed.'

'The shame, Hayding. The shame. It's anudder man ting.'

'But wait. Furder complication.'

'Shortly afterwards – the will of God according to the received wisdom of the time – your mammy had a hysterectomy.'

'The Big H. Bote parents infertile, which brought your dearly beloved aunties into the mix.'

'To wit ourselves.'

'And we know what you're tinking. Isn't that a bit incestual?'

It hadn't been what he was thinking. It was now. How much more chilling could one family saga get?

'Relax, Hayding. Dere's a biblical precedent – tink Adam and Eve – so it has the Almighty seal of approval.'

'Besides, it was all very discreet. Nutting fornicatious. They decided on Eddie's naughty stuff, artificial insemmilation.'

'Exackly. You were a test tube babby.'

'And besides, look at you. You turned out well, all tings considered.'

'Anyway, Hayding, one of us was the surrogate mammy. Only we can't remember which one on account of we tink we've got dementia.'

'Hard to tell any more. Could be just the passage of time's wingèd chariot. It plays havoc wit your mental facilities.'

'But the babby. No records, it goes witout saying. Ireland in those dark times, Hayding. It remained, until this very moment, a closed fambly secret.'

All three possible mothers beamed up at their equally possible son.

'So in conclusion, Hayding, there you are.'

'One dead da, tree mammies.'

'What are the chances of that?'

This set them off on a fresh fit of giggles.

Hayden glared at them. 'What? Why are you laughing?'

'Oh, nutting, Hayding. Stop it, Dottie.'

'Dodie.'

They continued to ripple with repressed mirth.

'You killed your da, Hayding. *Very* Oedipal.'

'Wait for it, Hayding. All togedder now, ladies.'

'Oedipal Schmoedipal. Who cares, as long as he loves his mammies.'[23]

And they were off again. Bordering on hysterical.

Hayden stood up and towered over them. 'Not funny. Besides, this whole story is patent nonsense. You're all well into your nineties. Work it out. You were well past it when I was, well, you know. *Conceived.*'

'Not so, Hayding. We may have lied about our age.'

'Difficult to remember after all these years, what wit the dementia and the passage of time from one millennium to anudder.'

'I mean, *everyone's* an octogenaireeing these days, so we may just may have tought – why not skip the eighties? Seventy-eight, seventy-nine, ninety.'

---

[23] Prof. Larry Stern, *Beyond a Joke: Comedy and Irish Mothers.*

'Real ages wit-held.'

'But to address the point at issue, Hayding. When you were born, we were fruitful and abundant.'

'Well, one of us was.'

'QED.'

Hayden sighed and sat down again. This explained why his parents had moved to Waikiki without him. They weren't his parents. Either of them. It must have been eating away at them all that time. No wonder they were cold and distant.

And – Eddie? Had he really killed his own father?

He put his head in his hands. Real head, real hands. The three aunts moved protectively closer.

'Ah, will you look at him, the craytur. What's the matter now?'

'There, there. Tell your mammies.'

'I – I don't even remember the trip over, let alone killing anyone.'

'I gave you a lift from the airport,' said Bram. 'Remember? I dragged you out of the Nautical Buoy at midnight. You were pretty Scrabstered to be honest. Dropped you off at Eddie's. Didn't see you for the rest of the week, until –'

Hayden shook his hands-held head. 'I don't believe this.'

The three aunts fell uncharacteristically quiet. Almost meditative.

'Believe it, Hayding. What was it the immortal bard said?'

'Oh, what a tangled web we weave...'

'... when first we practice to conceive.'

Bram chuckled quietly. 'Well, that explains the visits to your one anyway. The head doctor.'

Hayden ignored this. He looked, instead, at the three miniscule women d'un uncertain âge, all now beaming up at him. He was reminded of the French horror classic, *Les Tantes*, in which – but it didn't bear thinking about.

So he didn't.

33

H ayden is about to go through the dark night of the soul.
After the aunts and Bram leave, he draws the curtains
and takes to his childhood bed. He slumbers fitfully through
the witching hour, then slips into deep and disturbing dreams.
Example: he's a small boy. Marina is beckoning him into her
'treatment room'. Her choice of lingerie suggests there might
well be a bed in there. Hayden is terrified but simultaneously
captivated. He can't help himself. He enters, mesmerised. The
door closes. Marina has metamorphosed into the three aunts.
One body. Same lingerie. Stockings.

Hayden woke to the sound of a long, silent scream. He was
sitting up on the bed, mouth open, his face a mask of terror.
He lay back down, whimpering, and fell into a deeper, dreamier
sleep. In the morning, he woke again; bleary-eyed, washed out,
wan. A shaft of sunlight angled through the curtains and rested,
lovingly, on a bottle of Uncle Eddie's Sweet Amnesia[24] lying on
his small boy duvet.

This I found almost too much to bear. I, too, have known
the shaft of sunlight, the tempting bottle, the darkened room;
but not the phone call summoning our tragic hero to his final
humiliation. Hayden ignored it. Good decision. He was in no fit
state for further debasement. It rang again. He took it.

'Ay.'

Hayden was in no mood for name banter. 'Rich.'

'Last chance saloon, Ay. Fing is, Foetus won Manitoba
Comedy Festival's New Act of the Year Award, you didn't. Foetus

---

[24] The three aunts were right. I'd misread the label.

is hot, you're not. So. Tour. Foetus plus support. I tried Special Guest but they said, "Ayden oo?" Anyway, decent moolah, not great, what say?'

Hayden may have been going through the Seven Stages of Disintegration at this point.

'Okay,' he said.

'Triff,' said Rich.

End call.

Back to the shaft of sunlight, the bottle, the room. Uncle Eddie's Sweet Amnesia. Would Hayden succumb to its seductive blandishments? As he clutched the top of his childhood duvet, I could hardly bear to watch.

Hayden languished there for some time, attended by the sad-eyed, ever-faithful Rusty. The bottle, thankfully, remained full, the sun still illuminating its contents, but less aggressively. The angle somehow more muted. Crisis over. For now. Hayden groaned and stretched. He looked both agitated and stuporous.

He staggered over to the window, drew the bedroom curtains back, squinted at the light. He was about to totter back to bed when he spotted the thick brown folder on the desk by the window. It seemed totally out of place in a child's bedroom, so why was it there? He picked it up and took it over to the bed. Sat down. Opened it. It was full of clippings from the past. His, Hayden's past. Reviews. Publicity shots. An in-depth interview in *The Irish Times* when he'd first broken through. Eddie had cut them out. Correction. His father had cut them out. He'd cut them out because – because he was secretly proud of his only son?

Hayden welled up. Eddie had been looking out for his career from a distance, unable to ever admit to being his dad. He'd tried to guide Hayden in the right direction – he'd been right about the leprechaun suit ad! – and how had Hayden repaid him? The Oedipal way. He should have been too old for that, but there's no time limit on killing your father, which is exactly what Hayden had done. He'd killed his father. He felt a deep sense of shame and, suddenly decisive, he dressed quickly, grabbed his jacket, ignored Rusty in passing, slammed the front door behind him and set off down the drive. Pascal, around the side of the house, stopped pumping Eddie's tyres.

'I just killed Mammy,' he said.

Hayden didn't turn back.

'Of course you did, Pascal,' he muttered. 'Of course you bloody did.'

He set his face towards the Garda station, and didn't stop until he'd arrived and asked to speak to Detective Inspector Lou Brannigan about a subject of the utmost importance.

He wished to confess to the murder of Eddie McGlynn.

Lou Brannigan sat with his feet on the desk, poking at his ear with a toothpick. He flicked it at the bin as Hayden was ushered in.

'So, what's this about you and the bould Eddie?' he said, motioning to a seat. The tone was laconic, a suggestion of amused disbelief. Of having all the time in the world. Of waiting to be entertained. 'I suppose you'll be wanting to confess to a few more while you're at it. Help us clear up the books.'

Hayden sat down. 'Just the one,' he said.

Brannigan chortled genially. 'Makes a change,' he said. He swapped his feet over and sighed. 'Lookit, I admit I got it wrong about Eddie's mutt, but I like to think I know what's what vis-à-vis and relating to the criminal fraternity and, by inference, the world of crime. Let me give you a brief rundown of what *I* think, and when I've finished you can let me know what *you* think. See if we can't meet halfway.'

Hayden knew what he knew. That was as halfway as he was prepared to go. He sat low in his seat and shrugged. The whatever shrug.

'Good man yourself,' said Brannigan. 'Right, so let's see now. You're a bit of an oul gag merchant. You've had what I believe is called 'a chequered career'. That Tourist Board ad: the leprechaun suit job. Begod but that was the business entirely. And, so I'm told, you had a biteen part in *Father Brown's Buachaillí*. About twelve seconds be the sound of it. Apart from that?' He spread his hands and switched legs with an ease born of natural indolence. 'Now here's my theory on the subject. You like to step up there into the limelight and have folk look at you. Well why not, I suppose. It seems to work for some people.' His stomach rippled with suppressed mirth. 'Have you seen that Foetus O'Flaherty gent? He was on the gogglebox last night and by God but that lad is the business entirely. *Termonfeckin! Yow!*' He paused to ripple all over. 'Priceless. You, on the other hand, and not to dwell overlong on human misery, patently fall some way short of that exalted state. No harm in that. I sometimes wonder if I'm in the right job myself. But here's the exquisite thing. You can't let go. You crave the spotlight. You don't get it through the accepted channels, so what do you do? You manufacture a dang fool shaggy dog story with you in the lead role. Centre stage all the way. "I'm after going and killing me geriatric uncle who died of natural causes." And there you are. Celebrity guaranteed.'

Hayden felt the need to interject at this point. 'Father,' he said. 'Turns out Eddie was my da.'

Brannigan pushed his chair back in mock disbelief. 'See? Uncle isn't good enough for him. Oh no. Let's up the ante here. It has to be his daddy.' He leaned forward, ham fists bunched in front of him. 'Will you stop it now this minyute, because I'm here to tell you that one fantasist in the vicinity is more than enough for this particular DI. So damp down the ego there, sonny, and stop wasting –' The door opened abruptly. 'What is, sergeant? Can't you see I'm – well?'

The sergeant shuffled over and whispered in Brannigan's ear, his eye trained on Hayden to make sure he wasn't reading his lips. This was serious.

'Do you tell me so?' said Brannigan. 'Is that a fact?' He sank down in his chair. 'Well now.' He sighed heavily and pressed his hands to his forehead. 'Pascal O'Dea's mammy,' he said, his voice somehow smaller, more vulnerable. 'Propped up in bed with a hatchet through her skull. Well now indeed.' The sergeant leaned over again. Brannigan stared into the distance, a look of inexpressible sorrow on his big, round face. 'Do you tell me so? Madden's, is it? Is there no end to the man's gall? I suppose he'll be buying the mammy's tea as if she's waiting at the half-door with a sweet maternal smile, the blackguard.' He stood up, suddenly resolute. 'Get the Special Branch round to Madden's. Every available shooter. We're going in.'

The sergeant hurried from the room. Lou Brannigan sat down again, suddenly deflated. 'His mammy,' he whispered, as if for his own ears only. 'Is there no limit to man's depravity? Or are we poised on the cusp of a new dark age?'

Hayden said nothing. There was nothing he could say. He felt as one who intrudes on private grief.

Hayden wandered the streets like a lost soul. He *was* a lost soul. In one stroke of an imaginary pen, he scrapped his novel. Not that he'd actually started it yet, but still. Big decision. He was weighed down by the unbearable burden of guilt. Not Catholic guilt. He didn't do that sort. Not, for obvious reasons, Jewish guilt. Nothing against Jewish guilt. Jewish guilt is as guilty as it gets. It's just that Hayden wasn't Jewish. Never had been. So just guilt. Guilt in its purest form. Guilt because he was guilty.

He felt ostracised. He wasn't ostracised, far from it, but people felt the force field of self-loathing that enveloped him like a storm cloud. No-one ostracised him; he ostracised himself. But back to the guilt. The pure, non-denominational guilt. It looks everywhere to atone for itself. Everywhere and anywhere. Example: there are no synagogues in Clontarf, but if there had been, Hayden would quite unhappily have gone in and spoken to the rabbi. He would at least have had the pleasure of a more exotic form of self-loathing. But all Clontarf had to offer was the Catholic church. True, there's a beautiful Protestant church about two minutes' stroll from Eddie's, but as far as Hayden knew, Protestants didn't wallow in it. Straight to judgement day. Hellfire. Damnation. No need for the intervention of a third party and the levels of bribery that entails.

So the self-ostracising, pure-guilt-ridden Hayden settled for abasing himself, head down, with a penitential walk along the sea front. See where it led. And lo! It led past the Catholic church.

Hayden hesitated. It went against all his finer instincts, but he was, as I say, headed down the self-abasement route. Catholic church, self-abasement? Perfect. Or was it? What would Eddie say? Correction. What would his father say? Because this went beyond the possibility of absolution. He'd killed his father. If the law wouldn't punish him, he'd have to punish himself.

His mind was made up. He, Hayden McGlynn, son of his father, would end his life as he should have lived it. He would finally, and irrevocably, do the honourable thing.

Commit suicide.

Top himself.

End it all.

Put like that it did seem a bit final, a bit irrevocable, but that was the whole point.

Wasn't it?

34

Hayden wandered around Eddie's for the last time. As he walked slowly through the house and back garden, those same emotions that had affected him so deeply at the scattering of Eddie's ashes crowded back in on him. The love, the tenderness, the sorrow and yes, the idolisation. And the something he couldn't find a word for. The something not quite so loving. The dark, brooding, clenched emotion that drove him to kill his own beloved father. And oh! The sense of loss.

He let himself out and walked down the driveway, also for the last time. He thought about cycling, but that would mean leaving the bike at Dollymount. It didn't seem right somehow. He also had Rusty to think about. He felt bad about Rusty. He must have met him on his last tragic visit, but he didn't remember a thing. Too late for that now, though, and Rusty was better off without him. He'd attach his lead to the three aunts' doorknob. They'd be sure to spot the soulful-eyed little mutt eventually. Just in case there was any delay on that front, he'd leave a full doggy bowl there too. One of those two-bowl jobs – food and water. He'd just put it down and was about to attach the lead when the front door opened.

'Will you look who it is.'

'Howaya, Hayding.'

'We weren't lurking behind the door, by the way.'

'Call it happy chance.'

Rusty looked up adoringly at Hayden. Hayden looked the other way.

'Oh, will you look at that. Such adorayshing, Hayding.'

'But what's this? He senses someting. You can always tell wit a woof-woof.'

'He was like this when Eddie went.'

'Inconsolable, but dignified wit it.'

'Oh yes. Stiff upper lip trewout, although I do seem to remember a bit of ow-ow-owooing last ting at night.'

This set Rusty off.

'Ow ow owoooo.'

'There. That's exactly it. Clever dog.'

'Oh, he senses someting all right, Hayding.'

'And he's not happy about it.'

'Not one teensy bit.'

As Hayden walked down Kincora Road, he felt eight eyes on his back. His heart was breaking, but there was no going back. His course was set. On to oblivion and the everlasting blackout! Assuming, of course, the Catholics had got it wrong.

He turned right down Vernon Avenue, passed Madden's, and met Bram as he reached the sea front.

'The very man,' said Bram. 'Day off. Fancy a quick one in the Buoy?'

Hayden studied Bram as if for the first time. The open, artless face. The slight air of permanent bemusement. Bram was his best friend, had been since childhood, and this parting of the ways was breaking his heart anew. He clasped Bram's nearest hand in both of his.

'My dearest friend,' he said. 'My dear, dear friend.'

'Fair enough,' said Bram. 'Is that a yes?'

'No,' said Hayden. 'No, it isn't. It's...'

He couldn't finish the sentence. It seemed so... final.

'A no,' said Bram helpfully. 'If you change your mind later, I should be in there for a while. You know. Relaxification time. Cúpla scoops.'

Hayden watched him go. A happy bus-driver's-day-off whistle. A middle-aged-man-skip off the pavement, back on, repeat. Through the glass door of the Nautical Buoy and out of

Hayden's life forever. A catch in Hayden's throat, a heavy sigh, and onward; ever, ever onward.

He crossed the road and walked slowly along the promenade, the glorious summer sunlight mocking his dark, doom-laden mood. Every step he took would be the last step he ever took along that particular bit of the prom. He turned right down the Bull Wall towards Dollymount. Same thing with the steps. Last time. Over the wooden bridge, the water swirling and eddying, beckoning, below. He could jump off there, but what if it was only two feet deep? Excellent for comedy if you timed it right. Finlay Jameson had done just that in his final, aforementioned two-reeler, *The Suicide*: the one where his accidental head-first death plunge was deemed too funny to leave out of the final cut by the studio bosses.[25]

But this wasn't comedy.

It wasn't tragedy either. Yet. It would be, however, when he reached the last bathing shelter before the statue, took his clothes off and walked, finally and irrevocably, into the sea. That was the very stuff of tragedy. But not if he pre-empted the final act on the wooden bridge and landed head first in two feet of water, with a group of foreign students taking mobile phone footage to send to the folks back home and, beyond that, the world of social media. The ten million hits scenario. *Hayden McGlynn RIP lol*. Hayden walked on.

On his right-hand side water and, in the distance, the mighty beating heart of the metropolis. To his left, the Royal Dublin Golf Club, fenced off to protect innocent passers-by from the clientele. My own aversion to golf was referenced earlier, so I'll say no more. Besides, Hayden was soon past the perimeter. He'd just arrived at the two point five miles of glorious Dollymount beach, complete with dunes. On one of the dunes he could distinctly see a large crowd, much as you'd see on the eighteenth fucking hole. Sorry. Language. But this was outside the imposing,

---

[25] Slightly truncated end, so technically a one-and-a-half-reeler.

and hopefully electrified, fence. I mean, *golf*! Listen, if you've been reading this far and happen to be a golf fan, I forbid you to read on.

The crowd was hushed. A scene was being played out in silence out of view. What could it be? Not golf, surely, unless the more odious practitioners of that equally odious sport[26] had decided to extend the boundary fence by laying claim to the public dunes. Hayden's curiosity won the day. Curiosity first, *then* suicide. For obvious reasons, it wouldn't work the other way round. He prised his way through the crowd of hushed onlookers and there, leaning over a corpse, squatted Quilty, not a glass of single malt in sight. He was, however, swaying on his haunches and slurring ever so slightly.

'A contusion to the left phrenology caused instant death, Inspective Detector, which proves beyond doubt that he himself was the perpetrator of his own demise.'

The inspector clapped him on the back. 'You've done it again, Quilty. Drink?'

Quilty struggled to his feet. 'As well you know, old love, I never touch the stuff.'

They both laughed heartily and walked slowly, and possibly homo-erotically, away from the corpse.

'Okay, guys. It's a wrap.'

As the corpse stood up and brushed himself off, Hayden noted for the first time the discreetly positioned cameras. He moved quietly away. Nothing in this world, he reflected, was ever as it seemed. He made his way back across the dunes to the sea road and started walking down towards the statue of the Blessed Virgin Mary. Star of the Sea. The Brutalist-period statue that should have been Eddie's but wasn't. Just as *Father Brown's Boys* should have been funny but wasn't. Nothing was as it seemed; nothing was as it should be. Ah well. He'd be out of it soon enough. He'd go to the last bathing shelter, remove

---

[26] Before the introduction of holes, golf was played exclusively by existentialists. That I could take.

189

his clothes, walk down the steps and into the sea and sweet oblivion. No togs, but he wouldn't need them where he was going.

Ten minutes later he was down to his underpants. He folded his clothes neatly and worked his way, each step a final step on that particular step, down the steps.

Death, he concluded, was also a final step.

Maybe a bit *too* final, so he turned around and slowly walked back up.

35

Hayden had his clothes back on. He stood outside the glass entrance to the Nautical Buoy. Should he go in? Should he succumb to the grape, the hops, the other one? Barley. Anyway, yes and no. Yes, he should go in. Why not? He could wallow in misery in company. No, he shouldn't succumb. Why should he? It hadn't done him any favours in the past. Same with me. Drank. Stopped. The end. Not much use if you're writing a memoir about your personal battle with alcohol, though. Short book.

I realise I'm missing out on a potentially explosive scene here. The inner demon conflict. Hayden orders a pint. He sits struggling for what seems like years, but is in fact, let's say three minutes, glancing at the seductive froth before, in a nail-biting build-up followed by an ultimately cathartic resolution, he pushes the pint away, a free man at last, and orders a hot chocolate instead. Subliminal message? There's no inner demon with a hot chocolate, with or without marshmallows. But Hayden's only problem with alcohol, post-Scrabster, had been Trace and her insistence that he had a problem with alcohol. He didn't. He just had a problem with life. So in he went.

The place was Friday afternoon full. Several bar staff on the job. Voot O'Rooney had stopped singing about lunch and was now salivating, in the key of E♭, over *Sweet Pork Belly with Crab Apple Jelly,* neither of which was on the evening menu. And there, speaking of Trace, sat Trace. With Bram. Not to mention a large goblet of house white, as yet untouched. Hayden sidled over to the bar with his back turned, as far away as possible from Trace. But her voice carried.

'Anyway, there I am, Bram, in the local library.'

'I know, yeh.' That was Bram. Hayden's oldest friend in the world. Solicitous, caring, bus driver Bram.

'When there on the Staff Picks table, I see it. *Without a Trace.* I think, that's funny. My name's Trace.'

'I know, yeh.'

'Says on the back it's about this teen girl. Memoir type book, so I think why not? Get home. Large gin and it. Flick the book open. Top up the gin, least I think I do cos I'm totally lost to the world. I mean, it's heartbreaking, Bram. My heart is literally breaking.' She paused for a quick sob. 'Turns out –'

Hayden tried to tune out as he sat on a barstool and waited for Declan to come over. He couldn't deal with this level of misery on top of his own. But something made him listen on. The lure of a gripping narrative. *Turns out what?*

'Turns out,' she sniffed, 'turns out *I* was Trace. My twelve-year-old daughter had written a memoir about a mum who's never there. Who didn't even know she had a daughter till she read the book. Because that's what drink can do.' She was weeping openly now. 'But sometimes, just sometimes, Bram, it's the only way out.'

'Ah now,' said Bram, empathetically. 'Ah now.'

Hayden managed to catch Declan's eye and ordered a sparkling water. It was just as he suspected. Trace was about to embrace the Nought Point Plan, and it may well have been his fault. He'd rejected her, after all. He felt bad about that. He also felt bad about killing his father, so he sank into a morose reverie and examined the bubbles in his drink. They seemed so... happy. Rising up. Reaching the surface. Bursting. Life was so simple for a bubble in a glass of sparkling water, but not, it seemed, for him. He turned away from the contemplation of bubbles and glanced around. The swing door opened discreetly. Enter Quilty.

Except, hold on, it *wasn't* Quilty. It was the actor who *played* Quilty, out of character now but still dressed for the part.

Hayden was fascinated. It was that guy from – oh, he couldn't remember the film, but he was totally different in that. Ah. Got it. *East Clintwood*. Man rides into town riddled with corruption. Cleans it up. Everyone dead. Leaves. Brilliant. Wolfe Swift! That was it. Genius. The word was overused, but wow! And here he was, as himself. If it hadn't been for the Quilty outfit, Hayden would never have recognised him. Double wow! It was weird looking at him as not Quilty, not drunk.

'Half of lager shandy thanks, Declan.'

'Coming up, Mr. Swift. Been away?'

'You could say that, Declan. In a manner of speaking. Anyway, on to the next project. Short break and off we go again.'

'Anything lined up?'

Wolfe Swift took an exploratory sip of his drink. 'Couple of interesting offers, but I'm still on the lookout for the script that sings. Got one here as it happens.' He produced a sheaf of papers from a briefcase. 'Ah well, might as well take a quick gander.'

He sat at a nearby table and got stuck in. Declan turned to Hayden.

'Tell me about it,' he said.

'Sorry?'

'Come on, man,' said Declan. 'Shoot.'

Hayden was totally nonplussed. It was almost as if Declan could read his mind. Bit like Steve in London. Barman, philosopher, friend. He was even polishing a glass. There was something strangely comforting about Declan's manner. It invited confidence, as if he had all the time in the world. Hayden's defences fell.

'Well now,' he said, seemingly locked into the inevitability of it all. 'Where exactly to start?' He lifted his glass, killed a few bubbles, replaced the glass. 'My Uncle Eddie was murdered. I set about finding out who did it. Of all the people in all the world, the murderer, or perp, was the last person I suspected.' He swirled the bubbles round in his glass. 'But perhaps I should begin at the beginning.'

Wolfe Swift, at his nearby table, overheard the opening gambit. There was something about the way Hayden said it. The truth of it, the passion, the poetry, the pain, that drew Swift in, his grey, lupine eyes trained on Hayden as he told his sorry tale. No detail spared. No minor character left out. No twist in the narrative omitted. And what a narrative! What a cast! At the centre, Eddie, this magnificent, towering, neglected artist, murdered in cold, if protracted, blood.

Then the big twist.

'All that time hunting the killer in good faith and then, right at the bitter end, the unsuspecting detective unmasks – wait for it! – himself.'

An electrified pause. Declan shook his head in wonder. Hayden, drained by the intensity of the telling, felt a hand on his arm. Brannigan? Had the Detective Inspector finally worked it out? Had justice come to call?

He turned to face the owner of the hand. Wolfe Swift sat beside him on a barstool, riveted, his drink and script abandoned on the table. 'This is *brilliant*,' he said. 'Have you told anyone else?'

Hayden was confused. He nodded at Declan. 'I told him.'

'Doesn't count,' said Wolfe, grinning at Declan. 'He's a barman. Silence of the confessional.'

A group of young men crashed through the swing doors and headed for the bar, hooting.

'Hey fella, where you from?'

'Termonfeckin!'

'Yow!'

Wolfe Swift sighed audibly and fixed them with his piercing eyes. 'Keep it down there, lads, okay? The adults are in.'

Hayden was elated. Great put-down. He could work with this man. The kiddies dropped their voices.

'Sorry, Wolfe.'

'You're the man, yeh?'

'Thanks, lads. Cheers.' Wolfe turned back to Hayden. 'Now listen. Top movie. The private dick who doesn't know he's the perp. But with soul.'

Hayden worked this through. Wolfe Swift was right. Two reasons.

- The private dick who doesn't know he's the perp. Great twist.
- Wolfe Swift was always right.

Hayden lit up. The dark cloud of depression lifted. He realised, with an energising internal jolt, that he'd been sitting on his big idea all along. He'd cracked it by living it. *Huzzah!* 'Actually,' he lied, 'I'm halfway through the novel.'

Wolfe was energised too. He switched to work mode. 'The novel is dead.[27] Title?'

Hayden thought quickly. '*Bad Blood.*'

'Like it. Listen, my people, your people.'

'Bit of a problem there,' said Hayden. 'I've been so busy on this, I don't have people.' He got a brief flash of Rich. 'Well, I have people, but the wrong people.'

Wolfe Swift patted his arm. 'Trust me. When I've finished on the blower, you'll have the right people. Plus, I can get you a pretty decent advance on the script. How's that sound?'

'Well,' said Hayden, 'you know what they say. Your right people, my right people.'

'Good man. Thing is −'

'Hayden.'

'Wolfe. Shake.' They shook. 'Thing is, Hayden, I *need* this. And this needs *me*. Okay. Where can I reach you?' Hayden gave him his number. Wolfe Swift sprang to his feet. 'I'm on it.'

Hayden sat for a long moment, working this through. Wolfe Swift was right. It was the perfect story for our venal times. Man kills his father. Punishment? Success. Maybe this was Eddie from beyond the grave. His way of saying, 'You did what

---

[27] Now he tells me.

you had to do.' Yes. That was it. Eddie had lived by a simple mantra and now he'd passed it on to Hayden. The true artist is ruthless. Eddie forgave him. Better still, he applauded him. 'You killed your own father. Now that takes guts. Well done, son. I'm proud of you.' Hayden was quietly euphoric. Paternal approval. It doesn't get better than that. He drained his glass and stood up. He had work to do.

He spotted Trace on his way out, sitting next to Bram in front of her still unsipped drink. He'd totally forgotten about her in the excitement of the moment, and maybe it was the whiff of impending success, or the lure of the attainable, or maybe it was because he'd overcome those demons, but it was Friday evening and his guard was down; an explosive mix, particularly in post-suicidal man. There was something about Trace as she sat there cradling her goblet. A touching vulnerability, allied to her obvious infatuation. It could have been an excess of bubbles, but Hayden felt gay and jocund in the old-fashioned sense of the words. He melted towards her. Maybe Trace, after all, was the woman for him.

Trace and Bram were deep in conversation.

Trace fingered her goblet nervously. 'I wasn't there for her.'

Bram looked even more puzzled than usual. 'Where? Oh. Right. There. Right. There.'

He moved a hand across the table and slid her drink away. Their fingers touched. Magically.

'The thing is, Trace,' said Bram in that slightly put-on Dublinese that speaks to foreign women, hormonally, the world over. Something to do with sound waves, probably. 'The thing is, Trace, you've got to surrender to a Higher Power.'

Trace's hand moved slowly over his. 'Really?' she said. '*Really?*'

Hayden had intended to ask Bram for a lift to the airport but decided to leave them to their love mist. He left the bar, as countless heroes of their own internal narrative have done before him, a man alone.

36

A man alone. But a happy man. He strolled up Vernon Avenue, planning his glorious future. He'd move, for starters. His current London address was fine as far as it went, but it wasn't expensive enough for his new lifestyle. He, Hayden McGlynn, screenwriter, was on his way. He started plotting out the story in his head, adding a few details here and there. How the Pope Twins found redemption serving life for multiple homicide. How his double session with Marina hadn't been strictly business.

He whipped out his mobile. Punched in Rich's number. Waited.

RICH: Can't get to the phone at the moment. It's in my pocket but I'm all tied up. Leave a message if you think you're important.

Good. Hayden was going to enjoy this. The double-act answerphone message. Hayden. Hayden as Rich. He waited for the beep then spoke.

'Just a quickie, Dickie. Can't do the tour.'

'Why's that, Ay?'

'Well, Dickie, it's like this. Too fucking busy. Wolfe Swift, Rich. Heard of him? Irish "fillum" actor. Six Oscars. Wants to shoot my script.'

'Sweet, Ay. Now here's how we play it.'

'We? Nah, Dickie. Here's how *I* play it. First fillum, *Bad Blood*. Not about us, Dickie, so relax. For now. Follow up *Rich Mann, Dead Mann*. He kills his agent. That's you, Rich. No idea how to do it yet, but don't worry, pal. Hate will find a way.'

Hayden pressed End Call. He pictured Rich's face when he listened to it. Now that was very cathartic. He put his mobile on silent and positively skipped past Madden's with its crime scene tape, up to the corner, and left onto Kincora Road. He sauntered the last few yards towards Eddie's, singing internally at the top of his voice. He was toying with the idea of cashing in his double session with Marina when Rusty leapt joyfully into his arms. The three aunts spoke over his ecstatic bark.

'Howaya, Hayding. Long time, no see.'

'So how are tings in Londing?'

'And what, if we may make so bold, brings you back?'

Hayden peered over the cotoneaster. 'Eddie's funeral, ladies. Remember?'

'Oh God, yes. The funerdle.'

'What funerdle?'

'*The* funerdle.'

'Oh, that one. He left everyting to us, Hayding, by the way. In his will.'

'Well, apart from *Portrait of a Lovely Lady*.'

'He left that to Francis.'

'But everyting else he left to us. To be passed on to his only begotting son, to wit Hayding, in the unlikely event, it says here, of us predeceasing same.'

'He must've tought you'd die young, Hayding. You being a great artist and so fort.'

'Who did, Dottie?'

'Dodie. Eddie did.'

'Oh, Eddie. Who's Eddie?'

'Eddie is.'

They stared at Hayden, innocently but mischievously, over the cotoneaster.

'You'll have to excuse us, Hayding. We tink we've got dementia.'

'Stand well clear. It could be contagious.'

'Plus, we're up to here on morphine.'

Hayden walked briskly up Eddie's driveway, followed by peals of affectionate, possibly drugged-up laughter which, mingled with the melodious trill of the blackbird on Eddie's chimney and Rusty bounding up the drive after him, gave him a warm inner glow. A sense of peace. Of completion. Of all being right with the world.

He went inside. Put the kettle on. Sat at Eddie's desk, *his* desk, and planned out his routine. Writing in the mornings. Double session with Marina in the afternoons. He'd use the mother complex as an opening gambit and see where it led. Who knew, if the sessions went well, he might even get to smoke that cigar.

He glanced out the window at the luxuriant foliage, which seemed to Hayden in his current state to be life-affirmingly, vibrantly alive. The sun shone across Eddie's masterpiece, which now resembled nothing more or less than revered Irish screenwriter Hayden McGlynn.[28]

He opened his notebook. Blank notebook, blank page. Took the top off his Rollerball Needlevision TX20. Rusty sat at his feet, gazing adoringly up as Hayden began to write.

BAD BLOOD

By
Hayden McGlynn

INT. STAGE. NIGHT.

HAYDEN McGLYNN IS ONSTAGE.

HAYDEN: (V/O) I couldn't see the audience from the stage. This was good. I didn't want to see the audience from the stage. I wanted to be somewhere else, anywhere else, working on my novel. But there I was. Going through the motions. Again.

The kettle boiled. Hayden wrote on. The kettle could wait.

---

[28] Prof. Larry Stern, *Disquisition*, Chapter XXXIV – *Comedy and Self-Delusion.*

ACKNOWLEDGEMENTS

M y thanks* to Kevin Duffy at Bluemoose for his first response to the book, for publishing it, and for asking Annie Warren to edit. Perfect choice. My thanks to Annie for accepting.

Thanks to Todd McEwen and Alison Rae for valuable feedback at separate stages. Special thanks to Magi Gibson. Magi is a writer. I'm a writer. We live in a flat full of imaginary characters, and nothing I've written since meeting her has been done without her hugely positive influence. Editing, talking it through, in two cases publishing the finished product. Not to mention producing several Edinburgh one-man shows and overseeing my shift from standup to, well, this. If Magi has suffered for her own art she's certainly suffered for mine. Details available on request.

.

* All thanks heartfelt; but it's not the sort of word you can use more than once.